BENSON AND THE WISHING MACHINE

BENSON AND THE
WISHING MACHINE

Susan Dodd

Book Guild Publishing
Sussex, England

First published in Great Britain in 2006 by
The Book Guild Ltd
25 High Street
Lewes, East Sussex
BN7 2LU

Typesetting in Helvetica by
IML Typographers, Birkenhead, Merseyside

Printed in Great Britain by
CPI Bath

A catalogue record for this book is available from
The British Library.

ISBN 1 85776 959 7

For Dad and Mum

CONTENTS

1

A SURPRISE FOR BENSON

Benson, the ginger cat, strolled down the narrow one-way lane. He stopped to sniff the cool air and listen to the quietness. This was his favourite hour in Cinder Lane – no one to shoo him away, no cars to dodge, no big angry machines that collected the town's rubbish and best of all – no dogs! Benson padded slowly down the lane, hugging the shadow of the walls, just in case someone was coming to work early and surprised him. Past the yard where the angry rubbish machines lived. Past the scrapyard where the tangled piles of metal were kept, making weird shapes in the dull morning light.

Suddenly, the quiet stillness was shattered. Turning to look, Benson saw two large yellowish, shining, round eyes coming towards him, and heard the sound of bottles clinking together as if they were chatting to each other. Benson sat, out of sight, behind the large, old drainpipe that ran down a nearby wall, and waited while the milk float and its chattering load rattled by. With his two green luminous eyes shining, he watched patiently as the milkman left one pint of milk on the doorstep of Mr Elvic's workshop. Peace returned to Cinder Lane as the milkman turned left at the bottom and disappeared towards the town, taking his noisy load with him.

Benson stood up, stretched his legs and continued his early-morning amble. Past the back of the furniture shop and past the garage where all the taxis lived. Lights flickered on in the classrooms as he passed the primary school. The cleaners were going about their business of making the school a nice clean place for the children to come to. The lane was beginning to come alive.

Benson strolled past Mr Elvic's workshop stopping briefly to check that the milk was still there. Just a few more steps and he was at Bob's tiny cottage, which stood at the end of the lane where the main road ran. Bob's front door opened onto the main road, and Benson gave a small spring forward and stood on the high step outside Bob's bright-yellow front door. Benson's eyes roved over the town of Lud. There were roof tops of all shapes and sizes – some with chimney pots standing tall and others small. Wisps of smoke were beginning to curl from some of them as the town rubbed the sleep from its eyes and gently woke up.

As the sun rose, its rays began to catch the beautiful church with its huge proud spire soaring into the sky like a space rocket waiting to take off. The early bus rumbled by, carrying some sleepy-eyed people to work, and others looking as bright as buttons as they made their way to the market in the town.

Benson jumped lightly down from the step and walked back up the lane to Mr Elvic's workshop. He settled himself down on the doorstep to guard the milk. Mr Elvic would soon be here – eight o'clock on the dot – and that meant only one thing – BREAK-FAST! The marketplace clock began to chime eight o'clock. Benson looked up the road in anticipation – surely Mr Elvic wasn't going to be late. No, sure enough the familiar green car came slowly round the corner and into Cinder Lane. Purring with delight, Benson watched as Mr. Elvic parked his car in the yard next to the workshop.

"Now little fellow," said Mr Elvic, as he got out of his car.

Benson went to greet him. He purred louder as he was tickled under his chin by this gentle man who had rosy cheeks, grey eyes that twinkled behind glasses and an ever-ready smile playing around his face.

Because the mornings were chilly now, Mr. Elvic's mop of white hair was covered by a blue bobble hat whose bobble had fallen off and which matched his blue overalls. The workshop keys jangled as Mr Elvic took them out of his pocket. He picked up the milk and slid the key into the lock.

"Come on, Benson, let's get the door unlocked and get some heat on," said Mr Elvic.

Benson loved the workshop. He sniffed the familiar faint oily smells, and yesterday's fumes from the big black grinding machine still lingered in the air.

3

Mr Elvic switched on the huge gas fire that hung from the roof like a big umbrella, and then filled the old stove in the corner with newspaper and logs. He lit the paper with a match, and Benson watched as the flames flickered and danced around the log, waiting for them to burst into life as they took hold of the wood. Benson jumped, as he always did, when, with a sudden whoosh, the logs began to burn fiercely in the stove and throw out a lovely warmth. The flames were so bright that they cast flickering ghostlike figures around the walls. Shimmered reflections of the flames danced across the metal tools, lawnmowers and other machines that cluttered up the workshop.

"Here you are, Benson," said Mr Elvic placing a bowl of milk in its usual place – on the floor at the end of the huge, long wooden workbench. "I thought I might be late this morning because it's my birthday today, you know – the eleventh of November – and I had to open my cards."

The bench was strewn with every tool imaginable, but Mr Elvic knew just where each one was supposed to be. Under the bench were hundreds of bits of discarded scrap metal. He never threw anything away that might just be needed in the future!

"Time to open the office door," said Mr Elvic. He put the key upside down into the upside-down lock in the door. He thought that might help to baffle any would-be burglars.

Benson lapped his milk slowly, raising his head every so often to watch Mr Elvic.

"Better open the back door, eh Benson?" said Mr

Elvic quietly from the office. Carefully finding his way around the machines, he unlocked the padlock and drew the squeaky bolt across the door. There was a rush of cold air and Benson shivered. Mr Elvic disappeared down the steep steps that led to a small courtyard. In the corner of the yard stood a tiny building, built from dark stone, with a slanting tin roof. Mr Elvic put the key upside down into the lock, turned it three times to the right and twice to the left. He reached up, knocked twice onto the doorknob and the old grey door opened. Mr Elvic disappeared inside.

Benson had never been into the courtyard before and he didn't know what was inside the tiny building – it was a mystery and the unknown. He padded over to the wood stove and settled down in the warmth and cleaned his whiskers. The old clock on the wall ticked quietly away, and Benson's eyes began to close. As he dozed he could hear strange whirring noises coming from inside the small building. He had never heard them before and he began to wonder what was making them.

Benson was woken up by Mr Elvic gently tickling him behind his ears.

"I wish you could talk, Benson," said Mr. Elvic.

"So do I," said Benson in a strange, meowing sort of voice.

"Oh, my goodness. It's worked!" shouted Mr Elvic. "It's worked! It's worked! It's worked!"

"What's happening? What's happening?" cried Benson (in that meowing sort of voice).

"The wishing machine! The wishing machine!" cried Mr Elvic.

"Please, Mr Elvic, I'm scared," said Benson, his fur standing on end.

Mr Elvic looked at him. "Oh poor Benson, I didn't mean to frighten you, little fellow," he said. Benson's green eyes were as wide as could be and his tail twitched nervously.

"Come with me and I'll show you," said Mr Elvic.

2

THE WISHING MACHINE

With shaking legs and a rapidly beating heart, Benson followed Mr Elvic down the steps into the courtyard, and into the stone building with the tin roof. He glanced nervously around in the gloom. Large cobwebs hung from the low ceiling like grimy net curtains hanging in windows, and spiders scurried into the corners out of the way.

"There's sure to be a mouse or two in here," Benson heard himself say.

"Sshh! They will hear you," replied Mr Elvic with a hint of amusement in his voice.

Underneath a dim light hanging from the ceiling stood a small table with a weird-looking machine on it.

"I haven't seen a machine like that before," said Benson. "What is it?"

"It's a wishing machine," said Mr Elvic.

"A wishing machine? You had better tell me all about it. Oh dear, I'm still shaking. I still can't believe that I can talk."

Mr Elvic took off his bobble hat and ran his fingers through his hair.

"Well," he said. "It's like this. When I came to Cinder Lane about thirty-seven years ago I found a box in here covered with this old curtain. In it were bits of metal and pipes. On the lid of the box was written 'Wishing Machine'. I thought it was maybe a child's toy so I didn't think anymore about it. Here it has been for all those years until I came across it again about six months ago. I had a proper look at it this time. Underneath all the metal and pipes I found a scroll and some instructions ..."

Mr Elvic reached for a rolled-up piece of paper that lay close by and, having unrolled it, began to read its contents out loud:

"To the person who finds this machine:

1. *It is the only machine of its kind in the world.*
2. *Please follow the instructions and put the machine together again with love and care.*
3. *Only use the machine to grant good wishes – not evil ones.*
4. *Do not let bad people into the secret of the machine.*
5. *The machine will only allow one wish to be granted on the day it is used. This wish-day must be on a Wednesday, but when the moon comes up at night and catches the cockerel at the top of the church spire the magic will stop working. Anything already created by the magic will remain.*
6. *I grant one lasting wish to the person who puts the Wishing Machine back together*

8

again. This wish must be made on the first day the machine works again.

7. *I leave this machine in your safe hands and trust that in the future you will leave it in someone else's!*

The Wish Maker."

Benson sprang up onto the table to take a closer look at the Wishing Machine.

"It's just a tangle of old pipes," he cried, "with a handle on either side."

"No, no. Take a step back and then look," said Mr Elvic.

He scooped Benson off the table and tucked him under his arm, moving away from the machine.

"Ow!" Benson squawked. "Don't squeeze me too hard. You are always doing that and I have wanted to tell you for ages. Well now I have."

"I do beg your pardon, I didn't realise," replied Mr Elvic. "Now take a look at the machine."

Benson's eyes shone brightly through the gloom.

"It still looks like a load of old bendy pipes and metal to me," he said.

"It's in the shape of two letters – W and M. They stand for Wishing Machine," explained Mr Elvic.

"How in the world would I know that?" said Benson. "I can't read! Anyway, put me down now please, and do it gently. So, how does that contraption work?"

"It's easy. All you do is pull one handle forwards and push the other handle backwards, say your wish and the magic begins," explained Mr Elvic.

"Let's have a go then," said Benson, his meowing voice full of anticipation.

"Sorry, Benson, we can't. I have used up the wish this week by wishing for you to talk. You will have to wait until the next wish-day next Wednesday. Sorry, little fellow."

"Oh fiddle, fiddle! That's a *purr*fect nuisance. That seems ages away," sighed Benson.

"It will be here before you know it," said Mr Elvic with a smile that lit up the whole of his face. Even the wrinkles around his eyes seemed to be smiling! He tickled Benson on his nose.

"Do you know that can be quite annoying at times?" cried Benson.

"Oh really, you old moaner. Come on, it's time for a biscuit and a mug of coffee," said Mr Elvic, chuckling to himself. "I'd better cover up the machine with the old curtain."

He walked over to the corner where the old curtain lay.

"Goodness me," he said, "it's so dusty. It needs a good shake."

Mr Elvic shook the curtain and clouds of dust filled the tiny building, making them both cough and splutter. Suddenly, there was a loud bang and the room filled with hundreds of tiny lights shooting everywhere. The dust was turning into glittering stars of every colour on earth.

Benson took one leap and landed on his friend's shoulder.

"Woooow, what's happening?" he shrieked, wobbling violently and digging his claws into Mr

Elvic's shoulder, trying desperately to keep his balance. Mr Elvic reached up and stroked the terrified cat.

"It's all right, little chap," he said, "today is a very special day; because the machine is working again there must still be some extra magic about. Nothing will hurt you. Look what's happening – it's fantastic!"

Benson opened his eyes slowly and they got wider and wider with amazement. Hundreds of stars were dancing and twinkling all around the tiny building, looking like fairies carrying torches. Gradually they began to float down and land on the old dusty curtain that had changed into the most beautiful cover made of midnight-blue velvet. Both Mr Elvic and Benson stood transfixed in wonder as they watched until the last gold star gently landed into place on the blue cover.

There was silence, more silence and even more silence.

"Gosh! Follow that!" whispered Mr Elvic eventually.

With his eyes wide open and his legs still shaking, Benson jumped down from Mr Elvic's shoulder and padded cautiously over to the beautiful cover. He could not resist brushing the lovely soft velvet material with his paw, and as he did so the stars shimmered and shone again, sending rainbow-like patterns around the walls.

"I think we should call this old building 'Rainstar Palace'," purred Benson, his eyes shining with excitement.

"Enough shocks for one day. Come along now, I

11

really need to sit down and have a biscuit and a drink," said Mr Elvic.

He carefully picked up the cover and draped it over the Wishing Machine, setting the stars off on yet another twinkling flurry. As he turned the key to lock the door of Rainstar Palace, the last star winked, winked again and darkness fell. All was still. Rainstar Palace fell asleep.

3

BENSON HAS FUN WITH BOB

Mr Elvic slowly tipped up the flask and sent steaming-hot coffee into his black-and-white striped mug.

"Goodness me! I'm quite worn out by all that excitement," he said, sitting back in his black swivel chair.

"Soooo am I," said Benson, jumping up into the old armchair in the corner of the office. "Have you had a tidy up in here? It's not as messy as usual."

"I thought I'd better. Mrs Elvic said she would call in for a lift home on her way from town this afternoon," replied Mr Elvic with a grin.

"Yoohoo, Mr E., are you about?" came a voice from outside.

"It's Bob from next door. He's come to sweep up the workshop floor. Now you must keep quiet, Benson," whispered Mr Elvic.

"I'll think about it," hissed Benson.

"In here, Bob," shouted Mr Elvic, pushing the office door ajar.

Bob appeared at the door singing "Happy Birthday". He was dressed, as usual, in his baggy trousers with a big belt to hold them up, an old tweed jacket, a flat cap and the old familiar red-checked scarf slung round his neck.

"By it's getting chilly! I think there was a frost this morning," he said.

"No there certainly wasn't," said Benson.

"Who said that?" said Bob, looking surprised.

"I said I thought it was quite pleasant," spluttered Mr Elvic.

"Oh, OK, fine," said Bob, still looking puzzled.

"Would you like a mug of coffee before you start sweeping?" enquired Mr Elvic.

"I've just had one … but go on, another one wouldn't go amiss. Thanks," came the reply. "Come on, Benson, out of the way," continued Bob, giving Benson a gentle tap on the nose.

"Don't think you can push me around," growled Benson in that meowing sort of voice.

"Pardon!" Bob said, looking startled.

"I said, 'Why don't you sit down?'. I'm sorry – my voice keeps going all squeaky. With Christmas not too far away I've been doing lots of singing in the church choir – you know, learning new carols," explained Mr Elvic, glaring at Benson with those twinkling eyes.

This is great fun, thought Benson, but I think I had better keep quiet now. Mr Elvic looks rather cross with me. He retreated and stretched out under the office desk.

Bob settled himself down in the old armchair and picked up his coffee mug.

"It's busy in town today," said Bob. "I went down

14

earlier to the market to get my fruit and vegetables and you could hardly move. I was pleased to get back home again."

"That bad?" enquired Mr Elvic.

"Too right," replied Bob. "Thanks for the coffee. Time to get this floor swept. It didn't get done yesterday. Now where's that brush?" Bob got out of the old armchair and went through to the workshop. Underneath, and in the shadow of the office table, Benson's nose began to twitch and suddenly –

"ATISHOOO."

The noise made Mr Elvic jump so much that he twirled round twice in his swivel chair.

"It's so dusty under here," shouted Benson.

"Dusty under where? Where have you got to?" shouted Bob from the workshop.

"I said, 'These nails are getting rusty'." shouted Mr Elvic. "Be quiet, Benson, you are going to make me laugh," he continued in a whisper. "Bob will be gone soon – it's nearly his lunchtime."

"Are you talking to me?" said Bob, appearing at the office door.

"I was just having a word with Benson; I often do," replied Mr Elvic.

"I suppose you expect him to answer," said Bob with a chuckle.

There was a rumble of meowing laughter from under the table. Mr Elvic started to laugh, louder and louder, bending himself double and meeting Benson's eyes under the table. Benson stopped laughing immediately. Mr Elvic straightened himself up.

"I didn't think it was all that funny," said Bob. "I'm going for my lunch now. I'll see you later, Mr E."

"Cheerio, Bob," said Mr Elvic.

Shaking his head, Bob made his way out of the workshop.

"There's been some strange goings on today," he muttered quietly to himself. "Or is it my imagination?"

4

BENSON LEARNS TO SING

"Now then, Benson, I am going to nip down to the chip shop to get my lunch. I am not going home today as I am having a special birthday tea tonight with the family. Would you like me to bring you a piece of fish back?"

"Yes, please," replied Benson, "a nice piece of haddock will do nicely. I can't stand that cod you often get."

"You will get what you're given," chuckled Mr Elvic. "That's what my dear old mother used to say. Hopefully I won't be gone too long; it will depend on how long the queue is – it is market day when all is said and done."

"OK Mr Elvic, I'll have a snooze. It's been quite a morning. By the way, can I start calling you 'Mr. E.' like Bob does?"

"I suppose so," said Mr Elvic, as Benson sighed and settled down in front of the log stove that glowed so invitingly.

Mr Elvic locked the workshop door and made his way down Cinder Lane, turned left at Bob's cottage

17

and onto the main road. He waved to Bob who was sitting by the window eating his lunch. Whistling to himself, he walked past the small car park, turned right at the hairdresser's, down the hill, past the pizza house, tobacconist and Chinese takeaway.

"Oh no!" he exclaimed. The queue at "The Plaice" was out of the door.

"Oh well, I'll just have to be patient and wait," Mr Elvic thought to himself.

He joined the end of the queue of hungry people and his thoughts turned back to the events of the morning, and the smile began to play around his face. Who would have thought it? He had managed to make the Wishing Machine work again after all those years. Poor Benson – what a shock he must have had! And poor Bob! He knew something was going on! The smile got broader and broader and eventually he laughed out loud.

"Hello, what's amusing you, Mr Elvic?" a voice said behind him.

Mr Elvic quickly came back to reality and turned round. It was Ivan, the young painter and decorator.

"Hello there, Ivan. I've just had a bit of a funny morning, that's all," said Mr Elvic.

"So have I. I must tell you all about it," Ivan replied.

"Not half as funny as mine I bet," thought Mr Elvic.

"Well, I have been decorating the 'Woodhills' – you know, the retirement home just out of town, and ..."

Benson woke from his snooze, arched his back and

stretched his legs. He shivered. The stove needed more logs on it. The air was feeling chilly. Where was Mr E? He had been gone for ages!

"What a morning," said Benson out loud, "I can't believe that I can talk. I wonder if I can sing. Mr E. has been singing in the church choir for ages. What can I sing about? I don't know any songs. I'll have to make up a tune of my own. I know! It has to be about the Wishing Machine! If it wasn't for that I wouldn't be able to speak, never mind sing! Right, let's have a go."

Benson opened his mouth wide.

"Wwwhhhiiishhing Mmmaaacccchhiine ..." he yowled. "That was awful. I hope Bob can't hear me. Now come on, get a grip. Take a deep breath ...

Wishing Machine, Wishing Machine,
Helping people have a dream.
What other magic have you in store,
For people going through the Palace door?
Wishing Machine, Wishing Machine,
Helping people live a dream.
A cat who can talk, what a thrill,
It couldn't be more purrfectly brill.

Woooow! I can do it, I can sing," continued Benson. "I must practise and then I can sing to Mr Elvic when he comes back from the chip shop."

Meanwhile, down at "The Plaice", Mr Elvic was about to be served.

"The usual is it, Mr E?" said Jack from behind the

19

counter in his bright-white coat and white hat. "Pie, chips and mushy peas?"

"Yes. please, and a nice piece of haddock as well," replied Mr Elvic.

"Haddock as well!" said Jack in astonishment. "Are you extra hungry today?"

"No, it's my birthday and I am having lunch with a friend," replied Mr Elvic with a wry smile.

"Many happy returns," Jack said, "and how old are you today?"

"That's for you to guess and me to know!" chuckled Mr Elvic.

"OK, OK," said Jack, as he handed over the pie, chips, mushy peas and that nice piece of haddock. "That's £4.75 to you, Mr E. Thank you."

"You mean I have to pay for it as well," laughed Mr Elvic, handing over a five-pound note.

"There's your change, enjoy your birthday. Cheerio, Mr E."

"See you, Jack lad, bye," replied Mr Elvic with a wave of his hand, and he set off to walk back up the hill to Cinder Lane. He peeped through Bob's cottage window and smiled to himself. Bob, full from his lunch, was fast asleep in his armchair, head back and mouth wide open.

"I'm back, Benson," shouted Mr Elvic as he opened the workshop door. Benson sprang to his feet.

"Guess what! Guess what! I can sing. Listen to this ..."

"Not now, Benson. Let's have our lunch first before it goes cold. Talking about cold, I think I'd

20

better put some logs on the stove before it goes out."

Mr Elvic put three small logs onto the stove and then picked up the chips.

"Oh please, *please*, Mr E. I'll be quick," replied Benson.

"No Benson, I'm starving," said Mr Elvic, unwrapping the fish, chips, pie and mushy peas. "You can sing when we've eaten. There's your haddock."

He put the fish on the floor, and all thoughts of singing disappeared when Benson saw and smelt it nestling in its paper. He licked his lips and tucked in. There was almost silence in the workshop for the next few minutes ... The only things to be heard were the clock ticking quietly, the faint cries of the children playing at the school opposite and the occasional rustle of the chip wrapping paper as Benson and Mr Elvic enjoyed their lunch.

"That was wonderful," sighed Benson as he cleaned his paws and whiskers. "Thanks for the fish."

"Glad you enjoyed it. Let's put the rubbish in the dustbin," replied Mr Elvic.

"When you've done that, can I sing?" enquired Benson.

"Yes. I won't be a minute," said Mr Elvic on his way out to the dustbin. Benson sprang up onto the cluttered workbench to prepare himself for his singing debut.

"Away you go then, Benson," said Mr Elvic, stepping back into the workshop.

Benson sat up as straight as he could, took a

deep breath, stretched his neck and, with concentration written all over his furry face, opened his mouth …

"Rrrrrrrr, rrrrrrrr." The shrill sound of the telephone shattered the quiet atmosphere. Poor Benson nearly fell off the bench.

"Sorry, little chap. I'd better answer that," Mr Elvic said, going into the office. Benson heard him say, "Hello, Charlie, what can I do for you?"

"Just when I was up for my big moment," muttered Benson to himself, "that blinking phone had to ring."

"Oh dear, not again?" continued Mr Elvic, "I'll come straight away. I'll be with you in about half an hour."

"Oh flip! Sounds like Mr E. is going out," Benson groaned.

Mr Elvic came rushing out of the office.
"Sorry, Benson. That was Charlie, the groundsman at Grimble Town Football Club. The big mowers have broken down and they haven't finished cutting the grass on the pitch. They have got an important match on tomorrow, so I'll have to go straight away."

"But what about my singing?" Benson asked.

"Sorry, but that will have to wait until I get back. Now, are you staying in the workshop?"

"No, I'll go out for a breath of fresh air and stretch my legs," replied Benson. ("And have some fun!" he thought to himself.)

"OK, come on. Out you go," said Mr Elvic, grabbing his keys and locking the workshop door. "I'll try not to be too late, little chap – I must be back by five to give Mrs E. a lift home."

5

BENSON MEETS ROSIE AND MRS GEE

Benson sat on the doorstep and watched Mr Elvic's car disappear round the corner on its way to Grimble Town Football Club.

Across the lane the children were still outside playing in the school playground. Benson looked up the lane to make sure it was safe to cross, and then padded across the narrow road and sat down on the pavement to watch the children playing behind the wire fence.

"Hello, cat," said a loud voice, making Benson jump.

A little girl was crouching down, peering through the fence at him. She had a grubby face and a mop of tousled black hair tied up with a red ribbon.

"Hey, cat, what are you doing?" said the booming voice.

"I'm watching you all playing," replied Benson.

The grubby face suddenly froze the brown eyes widened like saucers, and the mouth gasped wide open.

"Did you speak, cat?"

"Yes I did, and my name is Benson, not cat!" replied Benson in a whisper.

"Wow! A cat that can talk! Goodness gracious me! I must tell Toby," squeaked the young girl. "Toby! Over here, over here."

"Noooo, you must not tell anyone else," pleaded Benson.

Too late! Toby ran over to join the little girl.

"What's up, Rosie?" scowled Toby. "I'm playing football. This had better be good!"

"Toby! Toby! That cat can talk and his name is Benson – he's just told me," said Rosie, quivering with excitement.

"Don't be daft, Rosie, cats can't talk. You've dragged me away from football to tell me that! Another of your made up stories," growled Toby.

"No really. I am not making it up … he really can talk," said Rosie, hanging onto her older brother's arm to stop him from going away. "Please, Toby, wait a minute and I'll ask him to talk."

Benson groaned inwardly to himself.

"I should have kept my mouth shut. Mr E. will be really annoyed with me for speaking out loud. I am sorry for Rosie, but I am not going to speak just for her brother."

Rosie crouched down, looking at Benson with those big brown eyes.

"Benson, say hello to my brother," she asked.

Benson stared backed at her, his green eyes unflinching and then proceeded to turn his back on the brother and sister.

"I knew that this was one of your daft stories. Wait

'til we get home and I tell Mum and Dad this one," said Toby. "A cat that can talk, I ask you!"

"But he can, he really can," said Rosie squirming, "I did hear him. Honest!"

"OK, if that's what you think," said Toby laughing. "There's the whistle – see you later, Sis."

Benson turned round to the watch the children line up, ready to go back into school. Rosie's face loomed in front of him, her eyes brimming with tears.

"Why did you do that? I know you can talk. I feel so stupid now."

"Rosie! Come and line up, the whistle has gone," shouted Mrs Brown, the dinner supervisor.

Wiping the tears away with her sleeve, Rosie ran across the playground to line up with her class-mates for afternoon school. Benson watched her go. He felt so sad. He had really upset the little girl and he hadn't meant to make her feel stupid … what could he do to make amends? He turned to walk back across the lane, pausing as a dustbin lorry rattled and thundered past on its way from the depot into town. Benson settled himself on the workshop doorstep which was bathed in weak autumn sunshine. He needed time to think. Suddenly, all of his senses were alert and his fur began to prickle. Benson's acute sense of hearing picked up the pounding of heavy paws on the pavement and the rasping sound of heavy breathing – and then his nose picked up the all too familiar smell!

"Oh help! Dowter has escaped again," he said out loud. "Where can I hide? He really likes chasing me!" Benson looked frantically around for somewhere to hide. "I'll try and get to Bob's backyard," he thought, getting quickly to his feet.

Too late! The huge black form of Dowter the dog came hurtling round the corner, his big paws bouncing along the pavement. He saw Benson and skidded to a halt. For a few seconds their eyes locked and both froze like statues. Dowter's large floppy ears suddenly flapped liked a pair of eagle's wings – the chase was on!

Benson shot across the lane without looking, with Dowter in hot pursuit. Neither of them noticed Mrs Gee puffing and wobbling down the lane on her rickety old push bike on her way to market.

"Look out," cried Mrs Gee as she swerved to avoid the animals. This made her bike wobble even more. "Oh! Oh! I'm going to fall!" In a tick Mrs Gee's large body bounced onto the pavement and her bike crashed to the ground.

Hearing the commotion Bob flew into the lane to see what was happening.

"Mrs Gee, are you all right?" he asked anxiously.

"I think so, Bob," said Mrs Gee, her fat rosy cheeks blowing in and out like balloons going up and down. "It's those wretched animals … oooh, where is my hat?"

"Here it is," said Bob, picking up the hat. "It's a bit squashed though. I think you sat on it!" His mouth twitched and he wanted to smile at the sight of Mrs Gee's ample body rolling about on the pavement.

"Now don't you even think about laughing at me!" she cried. "Mog on over here and help me up!"

She held out her hands so that Bob could pull her

to her feet. He pulled and heaved with all his might but nothing could move her from the pavement.

"For goodness sake, try harder, Bob," puffed the poor lady.

"It's no good, I can't pull you up that way," said Bob, desperately trying not to laugh. "Now let's try a different way. Lift your arms up."

Mrs Gee held her arms up and Bob went behind her and put his arms under hers.

"Right," he said, "on the count of three you push up with your feet, and I will lift you as hard as I can. Now, one, two, three – *push*!"

Bob heaved and Mrs Gee pushed. Slowly but surely the ample form of Mrs Gee lifted from the pavement until she was on her feet leaning against what felt like a soft cushion.

"Where are you, Bob, where have you got to?"

"I'm squashed against the wall behind you," came a muffled reply.

"Oh Bob, I'm so sorry," cried Mrs Gee, as she moved away from the wall and turned to face Bob. Then it was her turn to laugh.

"Bob, you should see yourself," she giggled.

His cap was perched on one side of his head, his glasses were all cock-eyed and his scarf was on the ground.

"Well, you should have seen yourself as well," retorted Bob.

They both looked at each other and began to laugh loudly.

"It's been a very funny day," said Bob, "now, are you OK, Mrs Gee?"

"Yes, thanks, Bob. I must get off to the market before the egg stall sells out. 'Bye now and thanks again." She picked up her bike and wobbled off down the lane and round the corner.

"'Bye, take care, Mrs Gee," Bob shouted after her as he turned back to his cottage. "I think it's time for a cuppa," he continued to himself.

Just as he was about to shut his door, Mrs Mawks came rushing by.

"Dowter! Dowter! Where are you, you naughty boy?" she shouted.

"He's up the lane chasing cats and has caused Mrs Gee to tumble from her bike," called Bob.

"Thanks, Bob. Is she all right?" asked Mrs Mawks in a worried voice.

"Yes, she's fine. She's got plenty of padding," chuckled Bob.

"Don't let her hear you say that," grinned Mrs Mawks. "Dowter got out again. I shall have to put up a higher fence – again! I hope he hasn't got too far this time," she continued, as she disappeared up the lane.

"Now let's put that kettle on," Bob said to himself as he shut his cottage door.

Meanwhile, Benson sat puffing on top of a tall bin in a corner of the lorry depot as Dowter leapt around it barking.

"This is all I need after the day I've had," thought Benson, "I've had enough of this!"

Dowter continued to bounce around the bin, making it wobble.

"For goodness sake, be quiet and SIT!" bellowed Benson. Dowter looked amazed and sat down obediently. "And STAY!" commanded the cat. Dowter whimpered.

"There you are, Dowter! What a good boy, sitting and waiting for me," said Mrs Mawks entering the yard. "Fancy making poor Mrs Gee fall off her bike – it's a good job she is not hurt." She put a lead onto Dowter's collar. "Come on, let's get you back home before you cause any more mischief, and leave this cat in peace."

Dowter took one last stunned look around the dustbin yard and trotted meekly after his owner.

"Phew, thank goodness for that," breathed Benson, "I didn't even see Mrs Gee, never mind realise that she had tumbled off her bike."

Benson made his way out of the lorry yard and headed back down the lane to Mr Elvic's workshop. Mrs Gee was puffing and wobbling the wrong way back up the one-way lane on her bike.

"Not you again," she chattered when she saw Benson.

"I'm very sorry, Mrs Gee," Benson said as she passed by.

"What? Who said that? I must be hearing things now. I must have bumped my head when I fell – I must be cross-'obbled. Oh dear, I'd better lie down when I get home," she stuttered.

Benson chuckled to himself.

"I'm having fun – I think. There's still Rosie to think about."

Mr Elvic had not returned when Benson wandered

back to the workshop. He shivered as a cool wind blew.

"Come on, Mr E. don't be too long now. It's getting chilly," thought Benson, "and I could do with having a snooze in front of the stove."

"Benson! Benson! Are you all right?" cried a voice. "I was looking out of the classroom window and saw you being chased by that great big dog. I have been so worried."

Benson turned in the direction of the voice and there was Rosie in the school playground. Once more Benson checked to see if it was safe to cross the lane, and padded across to the fence around the playground. A painting apron covered the little girl's dress, which was a good job as the apron was covered with blobs of paint in every colour you could imagine. Below the big brown eyes were smears of red and green paint.

"I was painting on the easels near the window and I saw what happened. Please tell me that you are all right," begged the paint-smeared face. Benson gazed intently into Rosie's pleading eyes.

"Oh dear me", he thought, "what do I do now? Do I speak or do I let her down again? Can I trust her with my secret?" Benson's thoughts were in turmoil.

"Please speak to me. I have sneaked out to see you. I'm going to be in trouble if I get caught. If you can speak I promise I won't say a word to anyone – even Toby," said Rosie, wringing her hands together. They were a glorious colour of purple paint. Benson made his mind up.

"I'm sorry I made you feel stupid, Rosie. I was

confused myself. I have only been able to speak today and I don't know how long the magic will last," gabbled Benson. "You must promise not to tell anyone, and if you see me tomorrow and I don't talk to you, don't be surprised. I seem to remember something about the Wishing Machine magic wearing off when the moon touches the church spire, and wishes can only be granted once a week."

"I promise, but what's the Wishing Machine?" gasped Rosie.

"Rosie Pemble, where are you? Ah, there you are. I thought you were washing your hands!" cried a rather cross voice.

"It's Miss Silver – my class teacher. I must go. Goodbye Benson, I'll be seeing you," said Rosie, and then added to herself, "Wishing Machine – whatever next?"

Rosie galloped across the playground and suddenly stopped. She turned and put a purple, painted hand to her lips and blew Benson a kiss. He replied by putting one ginger paw to his mouth and waving at Rosie. The little girl grinned and a few more steps took her safely back into school.

Before he had time to collect his thoughts Benson heard a car hooter being blown at the top of the lane. He could make out the green colour of Mr Elvic's car behind a dustbin lorry that was blocking the lane. Out ran someone from the bin yard, gave Mr Elvic the thumbs-up sign, climbed up into the cab of the lorry and backed it into the yard with its orange hazard lights flashing like zebra crossing beacons. Benson was waiting on the doorstep of the workshop when Mr Elvic pulled up and got out of the car.

"Hi there, Benson, the job didn't take as long as I thought it would. I expect you are ready for a warm by the stove," he suggested as he unlocked the door.

"Too right I am," said a very relieved Benson. He was so pleased to see Mr Elvic back, and thankfully ran into the quiet sanctuary of the workshop – he wanted a break from the big wide world outside. The workshop felt so safe and cosy. Darkness was approaching, and the embers of the log stove glowed in the gloom inviting Benson to settle in front of it.

"We need the lights on," said Mr Elvic reaching up to the switch, "I can't see what I am doing."

Benson blinked as the lights flickered on.

"That's better – now then, what sort of afternoon have you had, my little friend?" enquired Mr Elvic.

Thoughts raced through Benson's mind – should he tell about Mrs Gee falling off her bike, and what about Rosie? What would he say if he knew he had spoken to her, and, worst of all, had mentioned the Wishing Machine? Benson's ears flicked backwards and forwards as he thought about what to do.

"I think you had better tell me exactly what you have been getting up to," said Mr Elvic as he rubbed his chin thoughtfully. Benson slowly recounted the events of the afternoon and, when he had finished, Mr Elvic took off his bobble hat and ran his fingers through his mop of tousled white hair.

"My, my. You've been quite a busy boy, haven't

you," said Mr Elvic, ramming his bobble hat back firmly on his head.

"What about Rosie? Aren't you cross about what I've said to her?" asked Benson anxiously, his ears flicking backwards and forwards again.

"I ought to be, but I'm not. I know the Rosie you mean – it's young Rosie Pemble who lives with her parents and brother Toby on Lether Road, just round the corner at the top of the lane. They have had their fair share of trouble lately. Mrs Pemble has been ill and Mr Pemble lost his job when the sweet factory closed down."

"That's a shame, let's hope for better news for them soon," replied Benson.

"Yes, let's hope," said Mr Elvic. "Now, what have I got left to do this afternoon? 'Cos time is getting on."

Benson leapt up onto the bench near where Mr Elvic was standing.

"Talking about time," he asked, "did I hear you say the magic of the day wears off when the moon catches the cockerel at the top of the church spire?"

"You've got it in one," replied Mr Elvic.

Benson's ears began to twitch and his tail sank between his back legs. Tears sprang into his bright green eyes, glistening like raindrops caught by the sunlight. In a flash Mr Elvic realised what that meant and looked down sadly at Benson – for once the ever-present smile disappeared. He looked deep in thought and then realisation dawned. The smile flooded back onto his face.

"I've just remembered, I've just remembered," he yelled gleefully. "Come on, Benson, quick."

Mr Elvic grabbed Benson around his middle and headed for the door that led down to the Rainbow Palace.

"Owww, you're squashing me," howled Benson, "I've told you about that once."

"Sorry, we have no time to lose. Mrs Elvic will be here in a few minutes," cried Mr Elvic, "and more importantly, the moon will be coming out soon."

Benson was carried through the maze of machines on the workshop floor, his feet flying as Mr Elvic dodged his way around.

"For goodness sake, put me down," gasped Benson as Mr Elvic fumbled with the padlock on the door.

"OK, OK, but don't go away," puffed Mr Elvic putting Benson down none too gently.

"I'm not likely to with all this excitement going on. I'm far too curious," exclaimed the ginger cat.

The squeaky bolt on the door was wrenched open and Mr Elvic and Benson ran down the steps into the courtyard and to the grey door of the Rainbow Palace.

"Right, key in upside down, turn three times to the right and twice to the left, knock on the doorknob twice," muttered Mr Elvic to himself. In a trice the old door creaked open and they walked together into the gloom. Benson could just make out the bendy shape of the Wishing Machine with its beautiful midnight-blue velvet cover. The stars on it were lying still and dim as if resting before being woken up again. Benson shivered with excitement, remembering the magic moments from earlier in the day. Mr Elvic pulled the switch to put on the dingy light.

"Now where's the scroll that came with the machine?" he said.

"What's all this about, what have you remembered?" inquired Benson.

"Here it is. I'll tell you in a minute … I do hope I'm right," replied Mr Elvic.

"Right about what?" persisted Benson

"Benson! BE QUIET a minute," shouted Mr Elvic at the top of his voice. Benson sat down without another word. It wasn't like his friend to shout at him as loudly as that – it must be important. As Mr Elvic studied the scroll the wrinkles around his eyes began to smile.

"That's it, Benson, that's it," he said softly.

"What's it?" asked Benson, relieved that his friend had returned to his old gentle self.

"Look, the scroll says that the Wish Maker will grant one lasting wish to the person who puts the Wishing Machine back together again, and that this wish must be made on the first day it works again – and that's today! Don't you see, Benson? A lasting wish means that the magic will carry on for ever and ever, and not disappear when the moon comes up at night and catches the cockerel at the top of the church spire. Now, I put the machine together again, so I get this one special wish, and that one special wish will be that you will always be able to talk," explained Mr Elvic, stroking Benson under his chin.

Benson felt the fur on the back of his neck shiver with joy, his eyes filled with tears again, but this time with tears of sheer joy and happiness.

"You'll do that for me?" he whispered.

Mr Elvic nodded, his eyes twinkling behind his glasses. Two tears rolled down Benson's cheeks and splashed onto Mr Elvic's hand.

"No more tears. We have no time to lose," urged Mr Elvic.

He carefully pulled the cover off the magical machine and laid it over a chair tucked in the corner. A scattering of stars flew around the room but settled quickly down again, almost as if they were cross at being disturbed. Benson looked at the Wishing Machine with its tangled pipes and handles. He squirmed with anticipation, questions buzzing around his head. Would it work? Would the magic last? Would he cope? His life would never be the same again. Benson thought he would burst with excitement.

"Quickly, Benson, up onto the table," said Mr Elvic, breaking the silence.

Benson's ears twitched backwards and forwards as he took a deep breath and leapt up onto the table and sat down next to the Wishing Machine.

"I'm going to turn the machine on, and I'll want you to put your paw on that handle near you and push it forwards. I'll hold the end of your tail and the other handle and pull my handle backwards. Now then, ready? Nothing to be frightened about," said Mr Elvic, looking very serious. Benson just nodded – for once he could not speak. Mr Elvic put his hand around the back of the machine, and Benson heard a click. He then felt Mr Elvic holding the end of his tail.

"Benson! Your paw," he heard Mr Elvic say. He

quickly put his paw onto the handle nearest him and started to push. It felt warm to his touch. The machine began to tremble and make whirring noises, getting louder and louder. Benson's heart began to beat faster and faster. He closed his eyes and held on.

Suddenly … silence! Everything was still.

Benson opened one eye and then the other.

The Wishing Machine began to glow a deep red, getting brighter and brighter by the second, and just when you thought the light couldn't get any brighter it disappeared. Benson blinked and thought that it had broken down. He was just about to ask Mr Elvic if that was the case when the machine burst into life again. This time lights of all different colours lit up the weird machine, shooting round its pipes in all directions.

Benson looked on in astonishment and awe. Then he realised that the lights were thousands of shooting stars, just like the ones on the cover.

Then the whispering began.

"Wish, wish, wish, wish …" The words began to fill the room with their eerie sound.

Benson heard another voice – it was Mr Elvic's.

"I am asking for the Wish Maker to grant me my one lasting wish."

"Yes," came the whispering reply, "what is the wish you require?"

"I wish that my friend Benson the cat will be able to talk for as long as he lives," said Mr Elvic in a clear, firm voice.

Benson felt a tingling sensation shoot through his

paw. He looked around and gasped in amazement. The stars were somehow shooting from the handle, through his paw, down through his tail, up through Mr Elvic's arms and back through the other handle of the machine. They were joined together by a magical string of stars.

"Your wish is granted," whispered the voice again.

As Benson watched, the shimmering stars began to flicker and disappear as fast as they had come, their bright colours fading as they went. Mr Elvic and Benson were almost in darkness as they let go of the machine's handles.

"Woow! What a show!" cried Benson.

"Wasn't it just?" came the reply.

"Hello, Birthday Boy, where are you?" came a voice.

"Goodness me! It's Mrs E. ready for her lift home," exclaimed Mr Elvic. "We had better put the Wishing Machine to bed." He very carefully picked up the cover, trying not to disturb the stars, although a green one and a blue one decided to do a quick circuit of the Rainbow Palace, landing down as Mr Elvic pulled the cover over the Wishing Machine.

"I'll be with you in a minute, dear, I'm just locking up out here," called Mr Elvic.

Benson looked around. All was still. All was quiet. Mr Elvic pulled the old grey door shut, locked it and he and Benson made their way up to the workshop.

"Benson, no more tricks today. We don't want Mrs E. upsetting," said Mr Elvic in a quiet voice.

"No problems, don't worry. I've had quite enough excitement for one day," Benson replied as they emerged into the brightness of the workshop.

"There you are," exclaimed Mrs Elvic. "I've got rather a lot of shopping today. Are you here again, Benson? I can guess that you have been drinking Mr E.'s milk again and no doubt sharing his lunch."

Benson purred and brushed himself against the woman's legs – just as any normal cat would do.

"Come along now, Mr E. Time is getting on and we must get home. The family will soon be arriving for your birthday tea," continued Mrs Elvic.

"Yes, dear, I'll just check that the machines are switched off and the lights, and then we can lock up and go home. A drop more milk before we go, Benson?"

Benson gratefully lapped up the milk as Mr Elvic checked the machines and switched off the lights, making things safe for the night. He followed them both out of the workshop door. The air felt very chilly.

"See you tomorrow, little chap, hope you find somewhere warm to sleep tonight," said Mr Elvic as he locked up.

"Really, dear, you make too much fuss of that cat," said Mrs Elvic.

"If only you knew … if only you knew," thought Mr Elvic to himself.

As Mr Elvic climbed into the car, Benson turned and waved a paw, and then slowly turned and walked away up the lane. He was ready for a catnap. He hoped Mr Elvic would enjoy his birthday tea.

A while later Mr Elvic was waving cheerio to his family as they drove off to their home after a lovely family birthday tea. He paused before he went back inside. It was a cold, crisp night, and he could see the moon just catching the cockerel at the top of the church spire. He smiled to himself and thought of Benson.

Benson was sitting on Bob's front doorstep – he had been watching the moon for a while. As it caught the cockerel he threw back his head and began to sing:

> *"Wishing Machine, Wishing Machine*
> *Helping people who have a dream.*
> *What other magic have you in store*
> *For people going through the Palace door?*
> *Wishing Machine, Wishing Machine*
> *Helping people live a dream.*
> *A cat who can talk, what a thrill*
> *It couldn't be more* purrfectly brill.*"*

6

MR ELVIC AND BENSON ASK THE WISHING MACHINE A SPECIAL QUESTION

Like a shower of fiery rain, the grinding machine shot out sparks in all directions as it sharpened the blades of somebody's lawnmower. Benson kept well out of the way in his usual warm spot near the wood stove. Bob had swept the floor and was sharing a flask of coffee and a piece of birthday cake with Mr Elvic in the office. Rays of winter sunshine shone through the window at the rear of the workshop, catching the sparks as they ducked and dived in the air around the big, black grinding machine. Benson watched fascinated – he wasn't frightened of the black spitting monster anymore. He chuckled to himself as he remembered the first time he had crept into the workshop.

It had been a bitterly cold day and he was trying to find somewhere warm. He had sneaked in through the open door when Mr Elvic had gone out to put some rubbish in the dustbin. He had raced across the workshop and hid behind the black monster so that nobody would see him and put him back outside in the icy weather. He remembered his heart beating furiously as he listened to Mr Elvic walking around whistling to himself. Then the footsteps had come closer and there was the sudden sound of metal scraping metal, which put Benson's claws on edge. The machine began to shudder and sparks were flying all round his hidey-hole.

It became all too much for him and he thought the machine was trying to eat him. With a loud piercing MEEEEOOOOW Benson had run from behind the monster and jumped straight up into Mr Elvic's arms. Mr Elvic had stood holding the cat in amazement.

"Goodness, you didn't half put the wind up me making a noise like that. I thought the machine was going to blow up," Mr Elvic had said. "Now come along, little chap, stop shaking, you're quite safe," he encouraged, his large hands stroking the terrified cat. "Let's put you near the stove and get you calmed down and warmed up. I can find you a drink of milk as well."

Benson remembered being carefully settled down in front of the wood stove and being brought a saucer of milk. That's when Bob had arrived.

"Look what's just jumped out from behind the grinder," Mr Elvic had said with a grin.

Bob had looked closely at the ginger cat and said, "That's Benson. He used to be owned by Mrs Tutts but unfortunately she died not so long ago and Benson has been getting along by himself ever since."

"Well not anymore," Mr Elvic had said. "There will always be a bite to eat, a drink and somewhere to be warm."

Their friendship had begun on that day, and what a friendship it had turned out to be! Benson's warm memories were interrupted by Bob leaving.

"'Bye, Mr E., see you tomorrow," shouted Bob as he went.

"'Bye, Bob," replied Mr Elvic, turning off the grinder. The sparks disappeared to be replaced by wisps of blue smoke that floated around like ghostly shapes in the air as the machine cooled down.

"Did you have a good birthday tea?" enquired Benson.

"Yes, very nice thanks. Plenty of belly fodder," replied Mr Elvic.

"Belly fodder? What's that?" asked Benson.

"Food of course. All my favourites, and a special cake that Mollie and Susie helped their mum to make. It was a chocolate one decorated with Smarties."

"Sounds delicious. Those two grandchildren of yours are very clever kids," exclaimed Benson.

"They are indeed," replied Mr Elvic, his face lighting up with a smile. "I've brought you some cake – I'll just go and get it."

Mr Elvic disappeared into the office and came back with a small piece of cake wrapped up in a red serviette.

"There you are, see what you think of that," he said, putting the cake down with a flourish.

Benson nibbled the cake, chocolate icing sticking to his nose. He licked it off and his ears flicked backwards and forwards.

"Gorgeeeooous!" cried Benson, taking another bite.

"Glad you approve," replied Mr Elvic, beaming.

"Mr E., I've been wondering about the wishes and the Wishing Machine," said Benson as he swallowed his last piece of cake. "You and I can make all the wishes we want, but what about other people? It would be fantastic to be able to make some of their wishes come true."

"It's a great idea, but we can't let other people know about the Wishing Machine and its magical powers, just in case someone bad hears about it and wants to use it for evil wishes," explained Mr Elvic, rubbing his chin and frowning.

Benson looked disappointed and his ears flicked and his tail drooped.

"There must be a way," he persisted.

Still rubbing his chin thoughtfully, Mr Elvic said quietly, almost to himself, "There may be, little fellow, there may be." Off came the bobble hat and he ran his fingers through his hair; then he rammed the hat back onto his head.

"Let's go and ask the Wishing Machine," he said.

"But you've used up all the wishes for this week," squeaked Benson.

"I'm not going to ask for another wish. I'm just going to ask a question and see if the Wishing Machine can answer me," explained Mr Elvic.

"Let's go for it then," said Benson, his voice trembling with anticipation.

Out they went, down the steps to reach the Rainbow Palace. Mr Elvic took out the key.

"Now what is it? I'm so excited I can't remember," he puffed, his cheeks looking rosier than ever.

"Key in upside down, turn to the right three times and then twice to the left. Knock twice on the door-knob," shouted Benson as fast as he could speak. His ears flicked backwards and forwards again – this time with excitement.

Rainbow Palace was silent and still, and a shiver ran through Benson as he stepped in through the old grey door. He could feel the magic in the air. He heard the scampering of tiny feet as the resident mice ran for their mouse-holes and safety. Mr Elvic switched on the dingy light. Benson stopped and sniffed. He could smell MOUSE. His eyes glowed in the gloom as they flicked around the tiny room. Then he spotted it – a little mouse separated from its family, frozen in terror and its black eyes catching the dingy light. Benson crouched down and began to slither towards the mouse, which shut its eyes more and more tightly the closer Benson got.

"BOO!" shouted Benson at the top of his voice.

The tiny mouse squeaked as loud as a tiny mouse can, and a large spider came swinging down, dangling on a long thread attached to a huge cobweb in the roof, to see what all the noise was about. The mouse ran as fast as it could and disappeared, presumably to the safety of its home.

"You had me worried there, Benson," said Mr Elvic, "I thought you were going to catch that poor mouse."

"It's a good job I'd had that birthday cake," laughed Benson.

Mr Elvic removed the cover from the Wishing Machine. The stars stayed on the cover this time, rippling and twinkling their rainbow colours briefly around the walls.

"I'm going to do this myself, Benson, so you must sit quietly, listen and watch," said Mr Elvic.

Benson padded over to the chair where the cover lay and sat down next to it, his eyes fixed on Mr Elvic and the Wishing Machine.

Mr Elvic positioned himself in front of the magical machine and took a deep breath. He put his hand around the back of the machine and pulled down the switch. Benson heard it click and Mr Elvic then put his hands on the handles either side of the tangle of pipes and bars.

The machine began to tremble and whirr, becoming louder and louder – then as before, silence. Benson held his breath. The machine began to glow, redder and redder, brighter and brighter. Then came the whispering voice.

"You have used up all your wishes for now. What is it you want?"

Mr Elvic cleared his throat.

"Benson and I would like to share your magic with some other people who deserve to have their wishes come true. We know we cannot bring them here, and wondered if there was any other way of doing it," said Mr Elvic.

"There is only one way," whispered back the voice. "You and Benson must make the wishes for them, using the Wishing Machine. Then you must shake the cover and catch a star as they fly round. You must press the star into the palm of their hand and the wish will be granted."

"Thank you," said Mr Elvic quietly.

Benson watched in wonder as the red glow grew dimmer and dimmer and eventually disappeared. Mr Elvic stood quite still holding the handles of the Wishing Machine, still feeling its power.

"You OK?" asked Benson, rubbing himself against his friend's legs.

"Just a touch tired," replied Mr Elvic.

He picked Benson up.

"We can do it, Benson," he whispered, his eyes shining brightly behind his glasses, and the smile twitching around his mouth.

"How are we going to know what people's wishes are?" asked the cat.

"We will have to look and listen carefully – I am sure we will find out," Mr Elvic reassured him. "Now let's put the Wishing Machine to bed."

He picked up the midnight-blue cover and gave it an almighty shake. Stars flew in all directions like fire flies in the night. Benson jumped and sprang, trying to catch one but each time they avoided his flying paws.

"What are you doing, Benson?" asked Mr Elvic.

"Practising catching a star," Benson replied, "it's not as easy as it looks."

A blue star flew straight past his nose and he missed again.

"Wait until we have to do it for real," laughed Mr Elvic, "let them settle down now."

Eventually the last silver star winked and landed back on the cover. All was still. All was quiet. Mr Elvic locked up and they walked back up the steps and back into the workshop. Mr Elvic drew the bolt across the door that led down to the Rainbow Palace. He was making sure that the Rainbow Palace and its secrets were safe.

"Time to go home for some belly fodder, I think. Are you hungry Benson?" asked Mr Elvic.

"I am rather peckish," replied Benson.

"There were a few sardines and some salmon left over from the party. Will they do for you today?" Mr Elvic enquired.

"Lovveerrly," cried Benson, "thanks!"

Mr Elvic put the dish of fish on the floor at the end of the workbench.

"There you are. Get your tongue round that. I'll be back about two."

"'Bye, see you soon then," shouted Benson as Mr Elvic locked the door.

Benson ate his fish and settled down in front of the wood stove. He was full, he was warm, the clock ticked its tick, and he could just hear the voices of the children playing in the school playground. He wondered if Rosie was there. His eyes closed, he began to snore gently ... *and dream the dreams that only cats can dream.*

7

DOCTOR DOIT VISITS THE WORKSHOP

Benson was rudely awoken by someone rattling the door handle and shouting through the letter box.

"Mr E., are you there, are you there?" shouted a loud squeaky voice. "Oh dear me, oh dear me. What am I to do, to do? Mr E., are you sure you're not there?" the squeaky voice continued.

The peace was shattered. Benson woke up and rubbed the sleep from his eyes with his paws. Without thinking he shouted, "He'll be back at two!"

"Thank you, thank you, I'll come back at two, at two," squawked the voice.

Benson heard a car hooter being pipped. It was Mr Elvic returning from his lunch.

"Hello Dr Doit," called Mr Elvic, getting out of his car and unlocking the workshop door, "what can I do for you?"

"Oh dear me! They've done it again, they have – they've done it again! They've broken the teapot lid – dropped it on the floor again," squeaked Dr Doit.

Dr Doit ran Woodhills Retirement Home just outside the town, looking after elderly ladies and gentlemen. He was a very tall man, dressed in a very smart cream suit with a yellow carnation flower in his lapel. He had a long angular face, framed by a mop of dark brown curly hair partly covered by a straw hat. His matching dark-brown eyes darted around, taking everything in.

"It was Maisie Maddocks again," explained Dr Doit, waving the teapot around in the air. "The others dared her to do it. They didn't want to wait until the proper teatime, so Maisie crept into the kitchen to make a cup of tea, and what did she do? She picked up the heavy metal teapot and dropped it, dropped it, I say. It's the arthritis in her fingers you know – she couldn't grip it properly, dropped it, and the lid broke off again. What am I to do?" squeaked the doctor, his voice going higher and higher.

Mr Elvic ducked as the teapot was waved around again.

"All right, Dr Doit, let's get inside and I'll see what I can do," said Mr Elvic soothingly. "Again!" he added with a wry smile.

"I am so pleased to see you, so pleased. Your assistant shouted and said that you would be back at two," said the doctor.

"My assistant?" said Mr Elvic. "I haven't got an assi …"

He looked at Benson, who sheepishly slunk away, his ears flicking backwards and forwards. He was still feeling grumpy at being woken up so suddenly. He curled up under the office desk out of the way of the squeaking doctor whose voice was making his ears ring.

50

"Well someone shouted to me," exclaimed Dr Doit.

"It must have been Bob. He could have been outside in his back garden and heard you squawking – er, I mean talking," explained Mr Elvic.

"You got it right first time," came a squeaky voice from the office.

Dr Doit stopped in his tracks and turned to looked at Mr Elvic, the teapot swinging wildly from his long arm.

"I said it couldn't have happened at a worse time – the teapot breaking," spluttered Mr Elvic in a squeaky voice and going red in the face. "I was telling Bob the other day that my voice keeps going squeaky as I have been practising Christmas carols with the church choir."

"Oh dear me, dear me, that will never do! Now, head back, open wide and say *aaargh*," said Dr Doit, banging the teapot down on the workbench.

"No, no. It's all right now, thank you," protested Mr Elvic, clearing his throat.

"If you are sure," said Dr Doit, waving his long arms about, and wobbling as his long legs got tangled round each other as they frequently did when he got upset or excited.

"I just need to go into the office for a moment. Please excuse me," said Mr Elvic.

"Oh oh, now I'm for it," said Benson to himself.

Mr Elvic strode into the office.

"Be quiet Benson!" he hissed as he bent down to look under the table.

"Sorry, I am being very naughty," squeaked Benson, imitating the doctor again.

"Mr E., your voice has gone again, it's gone again! I am coming to have a look at your throat," shouted Dr Doit.

With his arms waving, he rushed into the office, got his legs into a tangle and banged into Mr Elvic who was still bending down looking at Benson. The impact threw Mr Elvic head first under the table and he landed on top of the astonished cat. Dr Doit skidded and landed with an almighty crash on the office floor, sending the swivel chair spinning like a top.

"Ow, ow, ow!" squealed the doctor as the chair spun round, catching his flying arms and legs.

"You're squashing me and I can't see a thing," yelled Benson pushing Mr Elvic with his claws.

"And you are scratching me," retorted his friend, "let me get up!"

Mr Elvic crawled out from under the table and straightened his glasses.

"Are you all right Doctor?" asked Mr Elvic as he brushed down his overalls.

Dr Doit was laid out in a heap, his straw hat was pushed down over one eye and his yellow carnation had somehow got stuck in his mouth. Mr Elvic felt a giggle brewing in his stomach. Oh, he must not laugh. Steeling himself, he helped the doctor to his feet. The doctor untangled his long legs, retrieved the carnation and straightened up his hat.

"Oh deary, deary me. Whatever happened?" he squeaked.

"You happened I think, Doctor," said Mr Elvic laughing. "Never mind, no harm done."

Doctor Doit suddenly froze and pointed a long shaking finger at the floor. Mr Elvic looked down and burst out laughing. His bobble hat was coming out from under the table. It had grown four furry legs and a tail!

"It's all right, it's only Benson. My hat must have landed on him when I shot under the table," chuckled Mr Elvic, carefully pulling the hat off Benson and putting it back on his head where it belonged.

"There you are little chap, we can see you again," said Mr Elvic, his eyes wide, warning Benson not to talk.

Benson wanted to laugh. Oh how he wanted to laugh! He could feel a giggle about to erupt. What could he do? He began to twitch, his ears moving backwards and forwards. He couldn't hold it any longer.

"*Meeoow, ha ha, meeoow, ha ha, ooooh, ooooh, ha ha*," cried Benson. He rolled onto his back, waving his legs in the air with his whole body giggling.

"Is he all right?" said Dr Doit, looking very concerned.

"I'm sure he is. He's just had a fright," said Mr Elvic, trying not to laugh. "Come on, Benson, let's put you near the stove to calm down."

He bent down and picked Benson up, who by now had tears of laughter rolling down his furry cheeks. Hugging the cat to him, Mr Elvic carried him over to his bowl of milk.

"Here, have a drink first," he said, putting Benson down. "Now Doctor, let's have a look at this teapot. I see it's the lid that's broken again. I can soon fix that."

Benson was still struggling to stop laughing and he spluttered into the milk, sending it spraying all over the workshop floor and his face.

"Do you think that cat should see a vet?" asked Dr Doit.

"I'm sure that won't be necessary," replied Mr Elvic, stifling a giggle as he concentrated on the teapot.

Worn out by all the hilarity, Benson settled himself down in front of the stove.

"All done, Doctor," said Mr Elvic as he unplugged the soldering iron, "it doesn't take long."

The lid was firmly fixed back on the teapot.

"Thank you, thank you," said the grateful doctor, "we will have to keep it well out of Maisie's way."

"You will indeed," smiled Mr Elvic.

"You'll send me the bill, won't you? Send me the bill," said Dr Doit picking up the teapot. "Goodbye now, Mr Elvic, goodbye."

"Cheerio, Doctor," said Mr Elvic, shaking his head and smiling to himself. He watched the tall man with the gangling frame leave the workshop, the teapot rattling about as his arms waved around. He walked over to where Benson lay snoozing and stood with his hands on his hips.

"What have you got to say for yourself?" he asked.

Benson didn't answer. Not even a flicker.

"You needn't pretend to be asleep," Mr Elvic said.

One big green eye opened and then the other.

"I really don't know what you mean," said Benson in a very squeaky voice.

54

"Oh don't start that again," chuckled Mr Elvic.

"I know I caused chaos," said Benson, "but it was rather funny."

"Yes, it was. At least nobody was hurt."

The remainder of the day passed away quietly. Various people popped into the workshop, some wanting to know if their lawnmowers were ready for collection, others wanting spare parts. PC Kedge, the local policeman, came in for a chat and a warm by the stove, as he often did.

Benson decided he had better behave himself, even when PC Kedge tickled him on his nose. He really didn't like that because the sensation made him want to sneeze. Just as Mr Elvic was about to lock up for the day, the door burst open and a bike appeared followed by a vision dressed in bright pink. It was Mrs Gee, huffing and puffing. She had her bright-pink winter coat on, a pink fluffy hat that tied under her chin, and pink wellington boots with white flowers on them. Her round cheeks were almost the same colour with the effort of pushing the bike. Her bright-red lipstick was the only thing that broke the pinkness.

Mr Elvic went to help Mrs Gee with her bike. He wheeled it in and propped it up against the bench.

"It's the pedals, Mr Elvic. They're all cross-'obbled. That daft dog and silly cat were playing chasing games up the lane yesterday and made me fall off. I thought my bike was all right, but when I got home the pedals fell off. *And* I have a big bruise on my rear end as well for all my trouble!" she exclaimed. "If I get my hands on them I'll … Oh, what was that?" she

55

cried. "Something ran past. I saw it out of the corner of my eye. Have you got mice in here?"

"I don't think so," said Mr Elvic, "you must have imagined it."

"No, no. I didn't," replied Mrs Gee, waving her plump hands towards the office. "It went in there."

"Well, I'd better take a look," said Mr Elvic. "You stay there. We don't want that lovely pink coat getting oil on it."

He went into the office knowing just where the "mouse" would be.

"Phew, that was a close shave," whispered Benson as Mr Elvic peeped under the table.

"I ought to tell her where you are," he whispered back, "then there would be a commotion. But we have had enough commotions for one day!"

"There are no mice in there," said Mr Elvic, emerging out the office. "I do like your wellies," he continued, trying to distract Mrs Gee's attention away from mice and animals. Her round face lit up like a full moon, her eyes like two shiny blue buttons.

"I found them on the market the other day – on that new shoe stall. They matched my coat nicely," she said, waving a chubby leg as high as she could.

"I shall have to tell Mrs E. about them. Now then, your bike will be ready tomorrow morning about eleven o'clock," said Mr Elvic.

"That's fine. Right. I'll mog on into town now. See you tomorrow," replied the lady in pink.

Mrs Gee picked her way carefully towards the door, reminding Mr Elvic of a large pink wedge of candy floss on legs instead of a stick. As Mrs Gee shut the door, Benson poked his head around the office door.

"Yes, it's safe to come out now," said Mr Elvic. "Poor Mrs Gee."

"Poor Mrs Gee? It would have been poor me if she had seen me," cried Benson. "I do feel a little guilty though," he sighed.

Mr Elvic glanced at the alarm clock inside the wooden case of the old clock on the wall.

"Is that the time? Mrs E. will have my tea ready!" he exclaimed.

Mr Elvic made sure the machines were switched off and the inside doors were locked.

"I'm sorry I have to turn you out in the cold, Benson," he said as he switched the lights off, "but you wouldn't be happy locked in here all night, and I can't take you home with me as Mrs E. starts to sneeze if she is near cats for any length of time."

"Don't worry about me. I'm fine cuddled down in the old armchair in the backyard of the furniture shop," Benson reassured him.

"Goodnight then, little chap," said Mr Elvic, bending down to stroke the cat, his eyes looking warmly at his furry friend. "Let's see what tomorrow brings."

He tried the workshop door to make sure it was safely locked and got into his car.

"Enjoy your belly fodder," called Benson as Mr Elvic flashed the car lights as he drove past. He watched the car disappear round the corner, its red brake lights flashing on and off. Then he turned and made his way up the lane. He could just make out two figures coming towards him in the early-evening darkness – one tall and one short. The short figure suddenly ran towards him.

"Rosie! Come back here this instant. It's too dark for you to be running in front of me on your own," shouted an anxious voice.

"Mum, I think it's Benson," called back Rosie.

"Just wait for me and we'll go and see the cat together. It may not be Benson and it may not be a friendly cat."

"Oh no," thought Benson, "it's Rosie. I hope she doesn't forget and go on about me being able to talk."

He sat down and waited as Rosie and her mum walked towards him.

"It's him, it's Benson," squealed Rosie with delight.

"So this is the talking cat Toby was telling us that you had met," said Rosie's mum.

Benson looked at Rosie. Today her untidy, tousled hair was tied back with a yellow ribbon, and she had obviously been painting at school again. He turned his attention to Rosie's mum. She was looking kindly down at him, her pale, slim face framed in blonde hair cut to the shape of her face.

"No, Mum, cats can't talk. I said that to wind Toby up," said Rosie quietly.

Benson nearly spoke with relief!

"Say goodbye to Benson. We must get a paper before the shop shuts, your dad wants to look at the job section," said Rosie's mum.

Rosie knelt down and put her arms around Benson.

"There, I didn't let you down. I told you I wouldn't," she whispered.

"Thank you, Rosie, you little treasure. Now off you go," whispered Benson in reply.

"'Bye, Benson," she said, stroking his back as she got to her feet again.

Benson purred as loud as he could and watched mother and daughter go down the lane, with Rosie skipping by her mum's side. Benson thought how thin Mrs Pemble was and then remembered that she had been poorly.

"I'd better go and stake my claim for the comfy armchair in the furniture shop yard before any of the others arrive. Bubble, Squeak and Zimba nearly beat me to it last night."

He quickened his step and squeezed through the opening in the fence. He was in luck. He was first. Springing up into the old battered chair, Benson wriggled around until he was comfortable, and fell into a contented sleep. It had been a wonderful day!

As Benson slept under the stars, dark shadowy shapes crept through the gap in the fence. Bubble, Squeak and Zimba were three cat brothers who roamed the streets and lanes after darkness fell. They, too, liked the armchair to sleep in at night. Silently, three pairs of yellow eyes glided towards Benson and the chair. The moon emerged from behind a cloud to shine over the sleeping Benson.

One by one, the three brothers leapt up stealthily onto the chair arms. Benson was suddenly alert. He could feel their presence and smell their fishy breath. He did not stir. He felt a paw push him, then another.

"That's not very neighbourly," he thought, "I'll keep still and see if they go away."

More paws began to push and poke him, becoming more forceful.

Without moving, Benson shouted, "Do you mind? I'm trying to sleep! Now SCAT!"

Bubble, Squeak and Zimba stopped in their tracks and looked at each other … humans in the yard at night?

"SCAT!" yelled Benson at the top of his voice.

The three brothers leapt from the chair. Bubble scrambled over the fence whilst Squeak and Zimba tried to squash through the gap together. They ran as swiftly as their legs would go, away from whoever was shouting at them.

"That will teach them. I would have moved if they hadn't started poking me," Benson muttered to himself.

Clouds covered the moon again, leaving Benson under a cloak of darkness once more. All was still. All was quiet.

Benson slept, *and dreamed the dreams that only cats can dream.*

8

A WISH FOR MRS GEE

At eleven o'clock on the dot, looking very bright in a multi-coloured poncho, with matching pink hat and boots, Mrs Gee appeared through he door.

"Good morning," she called.

"Good morning. You're looking and sounding very cheerful today," replied Mr Elvic.

Benson made sure he was well hidden behind the big black monster of a grinding machine.

"I am happy today," said Mrs Gee, approaching the workbench, "I dreamed last night that I was in a wonderful world of bikes – bikes of all shapes and sizes, hundreds of them. The most fantastic bike of all was coloured every colour you could think of, with a bright-pink basket on the front and a pink bell to match."

She looked at her old battered bike leaning up against the workbench.

"As much as I love my old bike," she said, wistfully stroking its handlebars, "I wish I could afford a new one. Still, I'll just have to dream on. How much do I owe you?"

"Have that one on me," said Mr Elvic, "it hardly took me any time at all."

"That's very kind of you," replied Mrs Gee with a big beam on her face. "Time I must be off, I can't stand here yapping all morning, the shopping needs to be done."

"Keep a sharp look out for cats and dogs," called Mr Elvic as she wheeled her wobbly bike out of the workshop.

As soon as the door banged shut, Benson came out from his hiding place.

"Did you hear that? Mrs Gee made a wish for a new bike," he said, his voice growing louder as he spoke. "If we can wish for a new bike for her, that would be marvellous."

Benson's eyes were open wide with enthusiasm, his ears going backwards and forwards in double-quick time.

Mr Elvic rubbed his chin and looked thoughtful.

"It would, it would. The back wheel of that old bike is bent and won't last much longer, and we are due another wish next Wednesday. You know what Benson? We'll give it a go my little friend, we've got nothing to lose," said Mr Elvic, his voice beginning to tremble with excitement at the thought of using the Wishing Machine again.

"Roll on next week," sighed Benson, stretching his back legs. "Time for a snooze by the stove, I think."

Mr Elvic fed the stove with several logs.

"There, that should keep it going for a while. Now I must get on with sharpening these hedge shears.

*   *   *

62

Benson woke early and shivered with anticipation – today was "wish-day" and they were going to use the Wishing Machine again. He stood up, stretched and lifted his head to sniff the cold morning air, glancing up at the pale, fading moon and the few stars still winking down at him. Stars! There were plenty of stars where he would be soon. Springing lightly down from the old chair, Benson made his way through the hole in the fence. Time for a wander before Mr Elvic arrived. He had heard the milk-float clinking its way down the lane earlier on, and heard it stop. He hoped it was leaving a pint of milk on Mr Elvic's step. He was ready for his morning drink.

Engines roared not too far away, so Benson quickly headed for his safe haven behind the old drainpipe. Sitting in the darkness, out of sight, he watched not one, but two dustbin lorries clatter past on their way to collect the rubbish once more. He waited while the shadowy shapes of Bubble, Squeak and Zimba passed on the other side of the lane, and then continued on his way to the workshop to wait for Mr Elvic to arrive.

As he neared the workshop he could make out the long shape of a car. There were lights on.

"What's going on?" he said to himself, feeling worried. "Who is in the workshop?"

Then a familiar figure opened the door to collect the milk. It was Mr Elvic! Benson ran to the doorstep.

"Oh, I was worried there. I wondered what was going on," he cried in a thankful voice.

"There you are, Benson. I couldn't sleep so I

decided to come in early today. Sorry if I gave you a fright," said Mr Elvic.

The big umbrella-like gas fire that hung from the roof was glowing brightly, and bright flames flickered from the wood stove. Benson's saucer of milk was waiting for him. He walked gratefully into the warmth and padded across to drink his milk.

"What I can't work out", said Benson, finishing his milk, "is if the wish is granted, how do we get the star into the palm of Mrs Gee's hand?"

"I haven't worked that out myself yet," replied Mr Elvic. "We'll just have to go along and see what happens. Well, shall we go and get cracking?" he continued, hardly able to contain himself.

"Ready when you are," cried Benson.

The door that led down to the Rainbow Palace was already open. Mr Elvic and Benson skipped down the steps. Mr Elvic quickly unlocked the door, nearly forgetting to knock twice on the doorknob. Once again the creaky door opened and they both stepped into the darkness of the Rainbow Palace. They heard the scuttling feet of the mouse family running for cover; it was too dark to see what the spider was doing – he was probably weaving his web and catching flies.

Without switching on the dim light, Mr Elvic moved to the Wishing Machine and removed the cover. Not a star on it stirred! Not even a tiny twinkle.

"You know what to do, Benson, get ready," whispered Mr Elvic.

They both stood in front of the wonderful machine. Benson put his paw on the handle and waited. He heard "click" – the machine was on. He felt Mr Elvic get hold of his tail, and out of the corner of his eye he saw his friend hold the other handle. The machine began to whirr, becoming louder and louder. Benson waited for the silence. Suddenly it came. Everything was still. The handle began to warm Benson's paw, and the deep red glow spread through the Wishing Machine, getting brighter and brighter – then as before it disappeared.

Stars began to shoot through the pipes, making Benson gasp, even though he was expecting it to happen.

"Wish, wish, wish, wish…" came the ghostly sound. A shiver ran through Benson to the top of his tail and back again. When the room was filled with its eerie sound, Mr Elvic began to speak.

"We would like to make a wish for our friend Mrs Gee. She desperately needs a new bike to ride into town on. We would like to wish for a new one for her," he asked in his clearest voice.

The air felt as if it was being blown around the tiny room, and the stars seemed to be darting faster and faster. Benson was mesmerised.

The tingling sensation began to tickle his paw. Stars were shooting from the handle, through his paw, through his tail, down Mr Elvic's arm and back through the opposite handle, as if they were joined together by a string of shimmering stars.

"Your wish is granted. Remember, you must catch a dancing star from the cover to complete your wish," the whisper came, echoing round the small building.

Their bright colours fading, the glittering stars dimmed and then disappeared, leaving Mr Elvic and Benson blinking in the gloom once again.

"We've done it, Mr E," said the jubilant ginger cat.

"Not quite," came back the reply, "we have to catch one of these stars yet."

"Oh that will be a piece of cake," Benson said cheerfully. "I did have a practice the last time we were in here."

"Did you manage to catch a star last time?" enquired Mr Elvic.

"Well, no … but that was just bad luck," said Benson.

Mr Elvic laughed, gently pulling Benson's ears.

He picked up the midnight-blue cover and shook it as hard as he could, and then laid it carefully over the Wishing Machine. Stars darted everywhere in a flurry, like a swarm of tiny, shiny bees, dipping and dodging around each other. Benson and Mr Elvic jumped and sprang, paws and hands stretched out, trying to catch a star.

"I've got one!" cried Mr Elvic. "Oh no! It's got away," he added, as a green star changed direction at the last second.

Try as they might, they couldn't catch a star.

"Mr E., the stars are beginning to land again," cried Benson.

"Try and catch one as they come in to land," shouted Mr Elvic, waving his arms around.

It was all in vain! One by one, the hundreds of stars settled back down onto the velvet cover. Green, blue, pink, orange, red, gold, purple and silver stars, stars of all colours, floated down until there was only one red star flying around. Both Mr Elvic and Benson made a last desperate dive for it. The winking red star landed on the cover – they had both missed it! They stood looking at each other in disbelief, disappointment written all over their faces. Benson's tail went down between his legs and Mr Elvic looked crestfallen.

"Oh no, we've let Mrs Gee down and we have wasted a wish," said Mr Elvic gently, his voice trembling as he spoke.

"I knoooow," wailed Benson, "what can we do?"

"There's nothing we can do. We should have given it more thought. We shall know next time," said Mr Elvic, straightening the cover on the Wishing Machine. As if to say sorry, the stars rippled with colour, briefly lighting up the room, making the tears that were running down Benson's furry cheeks glisten.

Mr Elvic picked up the sobbing cat and hugged him tightly.

"Come on, little chap. Don't take on so," he soothed his friend.

Benson wiped his tears on Mr Elvic's bobble hat and calmed down. Mr Elvic gently put Benson onto the floor. As they reached the door, Benson took one last look round into the dim, dusty room. Something caught his eye, up near the roof. Something was shining – something pink!

"Mr E.," he squeaked, "look up there!"

"It can't be …" said Mr Elvic. "Could it? Let's take a closer look."

He climbed onto the chair and peered into the dark corner. Benson heard a sharp intake of breath.

"It's a pink star caught in the spider's web," Mr Elvic exclaimed, hardly believing his eyes.

"Be careful, don't disturb it," called Benson.

Mr Elvic reached up and took hold of the star between his thumb and first finger.

"It's OK, I've got it!" he said. "Oh, oh, what's that?"

It was the big, hairy spider coming out to see what was disturbing his web. Mr Elvic began to wobble, this way and that, on the chair.

"Hang on, Mr E. Hang on," shouted the ginger cat.

He couldn't hang on any longer and Mr Elvic toppled off the chair with a crash, the star flying out of his fingers.

"The star, where's the star?" cried Benson.

"On the end of your tail," gasped Mr Elvic, getting to his feet. "Keep still!"

He crept across quietly to Benson and picked the bright-pink star from his tail.

"Phew! That was a close shave."

Mr Elvic looked at the bright star in his hand.

"Now where are we going to keep this safely until we need it?" he said, rubbing his chin. "I know," he exclaimed, and he whipped off his bobble hat, placed the star inside and put his hat back on as quickly as he could.

"Let's get locked up and go back into the work-shop. We can watch for Mrs Gee coming down the lane, though how we are going to get her to come in I don't really know," said Mr Elvic.

"I've an idea about that," replied Benson, as they

made their way up the steps, "I can sit outside on the opposite side of the road, and when she comes riding down I could run across the road a little way in front of her, and hope she is so cross she will chase me into here."

"It's worth a try, but please don't make her fall off her bike again," chuckled Mr Elvic.

"Don't worry, I'll be careful," said Benson. "I don't want squashing," he added with a smile.

"Now, now," laughed Mr Elvic, opening the door for Benson to position himself across the road and wait for Mrs Gee to come down the lane on her rickety old bike.

Benson glanced over towards the school and could see a hand waving frantically at him from a window – it was Rosie. He could just make out the light-blue ribbon tying up her mop of untidy hair. He raised his paw and waved back.

9

THE WONDERFUL WORLD OF BIKES

Hearing a familiar rattle, Benson looked up the lane, and there, in a blaze of colour, was Mrs Gee advancing on her bike. Closer and closer she came, her pink wellies getting bigger and bigger. Benson crouched down at the ready, then off he went, running across the road. There was a screech of brakes and Benson paused on the doorstep. Mrs Gee was wobbling to a halt, her pink wellies sliding along the road as she tried to stop.

"You stuuuooooped cat," she yelled, "I nearly fell off my bike again. Wait till I get my hands on you."

Benson scampered into the workshop and leapt onto the workbench near where Mr Elvic was standing.

"It's worked, she's coming after me. Get ready with the star," gasped Benson.

"I've got it, don't worry. I wonder what's going to happen," whispered Mr Elvic, "we'll soon find out – here she comes."

"You might well hide behind Mr Elvic," shouted

Mrs Gee looking flustered and wagging a fat, pink finger at Benson.

"I hope this works or I'm for it," he muttered.

Mrs Gee puffed across the workshop, her cheeks blowing up and down like a pair of pink balloons.

"Oh dear, I feel all cross-'obbled," she gasped as she reached Mr Elvic.

"There, there, Mrs Gee," he said, "do calm down. Come and sit down, now let me help you."

Mr Elvic took hold of Mrs Gee's hand and pressed the pink star into her palm.

Mr Elvic and Mrs Gee froze like statues. Benson looked on in amazement. A pink light began to glow around them both. Suddenly, they let go their hands. Mrs Gee opened her hand and looked in total astonishment at the bright-pink star she was holding. She opened her red lips to speak but not a sound came out. Her blue button eyes bulged as hundreds of coloured stars began to pour from the star. The stars began to fill the workshop with a whirlwind of coloured light. They began to swirl around the pair as they stood, beginning to form a long tunnel of brilliant colour.

Mr Elvic found his voice.

"Jump, Benson," he cried, wanting his friend to share the wonderful experience. Benson took a flying leap into Mr Elvic's arms.

"Wow," he cried, "here we go."

"Did that cat speak?" said Mrs Gee, also finding her voice.

Before anyone could answer, they found themselves tumbling through the tunnel of colour.

"Ooooo. What's happening?" shrieked Mrs Gee.

"It's OK. Just hang on," shouted Mr Elvic, stretching out his arm and grasping Mrs Gee's podgy hand.

On and on they tumbled, occasionally turning a somersault.

"This is great – *wheeee*," cried Benson, his fur flying backwards as they raced along.

"Ooooo help, I can't see," cried poor Mrs Gee, her skirt flying over her face and revealing a pair of pink bloomers that matched her wellies. She let go Mr Elvic's hand to pull her skirt down and went flying past the other two, squealing as she went and holding onto her pink furry hat with her other hand. Suddenly, the tunnel of light began to fade and the three travellers began to slow down. Slowly the light disappeared. They gently floated down and landed softly in a field full of brightly coloured flowers with petals that spun around like mini-windmill sails. Mrs Gee sat down with a bump, squashing a few unfortunate flowers as she did so.

"My legs have gone all cross-'obbled again," she said, dabbing her cheeks with a white handkerchief with pink dots all over it.

"Somebody please tell me what's happening. Where am I?" pleaded a mystified Mrs Gee.

Just as Mr Elvic was going to explain, a very tall man dressed in red trousers, a long stripy coat and a white top hat, rode by on the tiniest bike anybody had ever seen. It had two very small wheels and no handlebars.

"Welcome to the Wonderful World of Bikes," he shouted, waving his white top hat.

"That's it. I'm asleep. I'm dreaming again," declared Mrs Gee, "I'm dreaming about new bikes."

She huffed and puffed getting to her feet. The squashed flowers bounced up again, stretched their petals and started to spin.

"Shall we take a look round?" said Benson, "There's a gate over there."

They walked across the field of spinning flowers which gave off a scent of seaside rock as they spun.

"Mmm, smell that," sniffed Mr Elvic, "I love rock, especially the aniseed kind."

They walked through the gate and out into a long wide road. In the distance they could see buildings. Either side of the road were trees, but trees with a difference. The tops of the trees were completely round like huge wheels, with branches forming the spokes and leaves shaped like pedals fluttering in the breeze.

"Wow! This is quite something," chuckled Mrs Gee, beginning to enjoy herself. "Some dream this is turning out to be. You're very quiet, Mr Elvic."

"I'm taking it all in. I want to remember every-thing," he replied, his bright eyes dancing behind his glasses. Benson padded along between his friends – he hoped Mrs Gee would be his friend now.

"Weeeee, look out, look out," someone shouted.

All three of them jumped to one side – just in time. A silver streak shot by, leaving a cloud of dust behind it.

"Whatever was that?" exclaimed Mr Elvic. "It looked like someone riding a rocket."

"It was going so fast I couldn't see what is was," chuckled Benson.

"Look out," cried Mrs Gee, "it's coming back again!"

With mouths open they watched the silver streak coming back towards them. It was a silver bike with a small silver nose cone fastened on the front, giving it the appearance of a space rocket. The person riding the bike was dressed all in silver clothing, with a pointed helmet on his head. He was crouched down over the bent handlebars, and his legs moved so fast that they passed in a blur. The silver streak disappeared into the distance.

"I think we had better walk on the side of the road, or we are going to end up sat on the point of that rocket," said Mr Elvic.

They had just begun walking again when they heard a bell ringing behind them.

"Anyone for a ride?" called a voice.

They turned to look and saw a small boy with a cheeky grin, blond curly hair and dressed all in blue. He had with him a long bike with four wheels, three seats and a wooden basket on the back.

"I said did you want a lift into town?" he asked again.

Mrs Gee's eyes widened with delight.

"Oh please," she said, "my feet are getting so hot."

"Hop on then," said the boy.

"I'm not so sure," said Mr Elvic nervously, "I haven't ridden a bike for ages."

"Oh don't be silly. Get on, get on," twittered Mrs Gee. "Benson, you can sit in the basket," she continued as she scooped him up in her chubby hands.

"Ow, ow, just be careful will you?" grumbled Benson as he was dumped into the basket at the rear of the bike.

"Sit down and stop moaning," she said, heaving her ample body onto the seat behind the boy with the cheeky face. "Come on, Mr Elvic, we haven't got all day."

Mr Elvic reluctantly climbed onto the third seat and held on tightly to the handlebars.

"Right, ready. All push together, off we go," cried Mrs Gee, taking over.

They all pushed together and were soon riding down the wide road, picking up speed as they pedalled. Although Mr Elvic was clinging grimly onto the handlebars, he was beginning to enjoy himself. He liked the feel of the breeze as it whistled past, making his rosy cheeks glow all the more. Benson was sitting in the basket with his fur being ruffled and blown by the wind.

"Are you enjoying this, Mr E?" he shouted to his friend in front of him.

"Yes, but I wish we were not going quite so fast," Mr Elvic replied.

"Then stop pedalling," whispered Benson in his ear, "they will never know – you are at the back."

"What a good idea!" chuckled Mr Elvic.

He took his feet off the pedals and stuck his legs out wide. Now he was really having a good time.

There was a whoosh as the silver rocket flew past them again.

"My goodness," exclaimed Mrs Gee, "doesn't he ever stop?"

"He rides up and down like that all day," called the boy from the front.

As they rode into the town, Mrs Gee gave a shriek of delight.

"Look at all these bikes, just look at them all, Mr Elvic," she cried.

They climbed off the bike and thanked the boy for the lift. Mrs Gee looked at Mr Elvic.

"The last part of that ride was very hard going," she said. "If I didn't know you better I would have said that you had stopped pedalling."

Benson stifled a giggle.

"Look over there," he said pointing, "that's what we could do with."

Mrs Gee immediately forgot what she was saying when she saw the ice-cream seller across the road. The seller's bike was bright red, with a red-and-white umbrella to help keep the ice cream cool. Mrs Gee bustled across the road, closely followed by her friends.

"Ice cream! Ice cream! Vanilla, strawberry and chocolate," shouted the lady, looking smart in her white coat and straw hat. Mrs Gee and Mr Elvic both chose a strawberry flavour while Benson asked for chocolate. The ice cream came in big cones with chocolate flakes on top in the shape of a bike, with wheels made from brightly coloured sweets.

"Let's go and sit over there," said Mr Elvic, pointing to a bench and carrying Benson's ice cream, "then we can watch and see what's going on."

They made their way through the throng of bikes and sat down thankfully on the bench. They were ready for a rest. Mr Elvic placed Benson's ice cream in his front paws and then turned his attention to his own. Whilst eating, they gazed around them. They saw what appeared to be a large square filled with every different type of bike you could imagine.

There were bikes with one wheel, others with two, three or four wheels. Some had straight handlebars, others had bent or dropped ones. Some had tyres of all different colours, some had bells, some had hooters, others had baskets and others had saddle bags. Chains of all different colours rode by. Some had pedals that flashed as they moved. Everywhere the three of them looked they saw a different bike – no two were the same.

"This is wonderful," sighed Mrs Gee, enjoying her ice cream and taking in the sights. Into the square rode the tall man on the tiny bike that they had seen when they first arrived.

"Come along, roll up, the bike parade is about to begin in the Big Top," he shouted. "Follow me!"

People cheered and rode their bikes after him.

"Shall we follow?" asked Benson.

Mrs Gee was on her feet.

"Yes, yes, we must," she cried excitedly.

The three of them followed the bikes round the tiny, narrow streets. First they went this way and then that. At times they had to run to keep up. At last they came to a clearing and gasped. There stood the Big Top – a huge gold-and-blue striped tent with a bike on the top, lit up with flashing silver lights.

Benson's ears flicked backwards and forwards,

Mr Elvic rubbed his chin and Mrs Gee beamed all over her big face.

"Quick, let's get inside," she called.

Mr Elvic gently picked Benson up out of harm's way – he didn't want him run over. They walked into the huge tent and found a seat on the front row. The inside of the tent was a deep blue with silver lights twinkling all around, reminding Benson of the cover on the Wishing Machine. As the last person settled into their seat, the lights went out. A murmur of anticipation rippled around the tent. Then the spotlight came on to light up the tall man with the stripy coat and white top hat.

"Welcome, welcome," he cried, "to the Circus of Wonderful Bikes."

Everyone clapped and cheered. Benson sat on Mr Elvic's knee – he didn't know if he liked all the noise. Mrs Gee was cheering louder than anyone else.

"Let the parade begin," shouted the ring-master.

There was a fanfare of trumpets, which made Benson jump. Mr Elvic stroked him and held him tightly. The bright lights came on, the band began to play, the curtain drew back and in they came. Riders that had been riding in the square came into the ring, they were hooting hooters, ringing bells, waving brightly coloured flags, carrying balloons and blowing whistles. On and on they came, making their way slowly around the huge circus ring. Clowns were riding their one-wheeled bikes. Benson peeped out. He had never seen people before with white faces, red noses and brightly coloured hair. They were dressed in funny clothes and had flowers sticking out of their hats. He wondered why they were squirting water at people and making them laugh. He didn't think it funny when people threw water at him when he was walking through their gardens.

Eventually, the leaders of the parade made their way round the ring and were disappearing through the curtain. Just as the last one was about to go, there was a whoosh and a flash of silver as the rocket man roared into the Big Top. He powered his way twice around the ring before shooting off again, with the cheers of the crowd ringing in his silver helmet. To a roll of the drums the ring-master appeared again.

"Ladies, gentlemen, girls and boys ..." he cried.

"What about cats?" a voice shouted.

"Benson! Shush!" said Mr Elvic.

"... We have our exciting high-wire act now," continued the ring-master, "with our new and latest bike. Whoever dares to ride the bike across the wire will win it."

A gasp went round the spectators.

The bright spotlight zoomed into the roof of the Big Top to reveal the new bike. There it stood high in all its glory – a bike of every colour you could think of, with a bright-pink basket and bell to match.

"That's my bike! That's my dream bike!" shrieked Mrs Gee, waving her arms around.

"Thank you, we have our volunteer right over here," said the ring-master.

The spotlight lit Mrs Gee up with her ample figure, pink fluffy hat, pink coat and, by this time, very pink face. Some of the spectators began to titter; others remained silent.

"Mrs Gee, you can't do that," hissed Mr Elvic.

By this time the ring-master was helping an astonished Mrs Gee into the ring, her red mouth opening and shutting like a goldfish's.

"Mr E., dooooo something," cried Benson.

"What a brave lady! Give her a big round of applause," cried the ring-master.

"I can't do anything now. It's too late," answered Mr Elvic.

While some people gave Mrs Gee a polite round of applause, others laughed or remained silent.

"She'll never do it," they heard them say.

"Mrs Gee, whatever have we done to you!" said Mr Elvic to Benson, who felt tears pricking at his eyes.

Mrs Gee was having trouble climbing the fifty steps up the ladder to reach the high-wire platform and the bike of her dreams. She was shaking so much that her pink wellies kept slipping on the steps, and her chubby knees trembled.

"What am I doing, what am I doing?" she kept on asking herself.

At last she reached the platform where the bike was ready for her to cross the wire. She glanced down and shuddered, seeing a sea of faces looking back at her.

"I hope they can't see my bloomers," she thought.

She looked at the beautiful bike with its pink basket and bell. In the middle of the bell twinkled the pink star. Mrs Gee put her finger on it – it felt warm to her touch. A surge of strength went through her shaking body.

"I can do this," she thought. "I'll teach them to laugh and snigger at me."

She struggled onto the seat. There was silence, and then a loud trumpet fanfare made Mrs Gee jump so much that she landed back onto the platform showing her bright pink bloomers to everybody. There was a huge roar of laughter from the spectators below. Mr Elvic and Benson could not bear to look up any longer. Then everyone took a sharp intake of breath at the same time. Benson opened one eye and looked up.

"Mr E., looook!" he gasped.

Hardly daring to, Mr Elvic slowly looked up.

Mrs Gee was back on her bike and was slowly pedalling her way across the high wire. You could hear a pin drop – everyone was holding their breath. Every face was upturned. No one was laughing now.

"Come on, Mrs Gee. You can do it," whispered Mr Elvic, "you can do it."

Suddenly she began to wobble, her foot slipping off one of the pedals.

"Oh no, I need help," said Mrs Gee, putting her finger on the shining pink star again. She felt warmth, confidence and strength flow through her again.

"Come on, get a grip," she said fiercely to herself.

Slowly but surely she got the bike under control again. Her foot back on the pedal, she carried on across the wire. All eyes below followed her. Mr Elvic was clutching Benson so tightly that he was squashing him, but Benson didn't care.

Mrs Gee watched the platform getting nearer and nearer, then she was there! The spectators went mad, shouting, cheering and clapping. Then to the amazement of everyone, Mrs Gee turned the bike round and rode across the wire again, even daring to wave!

Mr Elvic was so relieved that he jumped into the ring and ran with the shaking Benson to the ladder that led up to the platform. Benson curled round his shoulders as Mr Elvic climbed the ladder to Mrs Gee, who stood there jumping for joy and making the whole platform shake.

"I've won it! I've won it!" she shouted as Mr Elvic and Benson arrived on the platform.

"Well done, but you frightened us to bits," said Mr Elvic, his eyes shining with delight and pride.

"Come on, get on behind me. Benson, you get in the basket," cried Mrs Gee.

"I don't think so," stuttered Mr Elvic.

"Oh come on, don't be afraid," she said, and picked up the astonished Benson and plonked him in the basket. Reluctantly, Mr Elvic climbed on the bike.

"Off we go," continued Mrs Gee with a flourish.

The noise got louder and louder, people were cheering and clapping. Suddenly, they were falling towards the white upturned faces of the spectators – falling, falling, falling. Then with a burst of shimmering lights they were back in the tunnel that had brought them here.

"Hang on to that bike," shouted Mr Elvic to Mrs Gee, "we're on our way home."

Benson swooped and whooped as their journey

continued, his tail streaming out behind him. Mr Elvic just went with the flow. The light began to dim and fade.

"We're nearly back," called Mr Elvic, "get ready for the landing."

The tunnel of light vanished and they found themselves floating down to the floor of the workshop, Mrs Gee still on her bike! They landed and all looked at each other. Mr Elvic and Benson burst out laughing.

"It's magic, real magic," spluttered Benson. "What an adventure!"

"You mean I'm not dreaming? All that really happened and you can talk?" said Mrs Gee in bewilderment, leaning her bike against the bench.

"Yes. We have a wonderful Wishing Machine, and we wished for a new bike for you and there it is," explained Mr Elvic. "Benson, just pop out and look at the moon and the church," he said, winking at the ginger cat.

He opened the workshop door and let Benson out.

"I still can't believe it. You did this for me? I won't be cross with Benson anymore after this," said Mrs Gee, shaking her head.

Benson sniffed the air thinking it was good to be back. He walked to the end of the lane, sprang up on to Bob's doorstep and looked up to the magnificent church spire. He sat quietly for a few minutes watching the moon, then made the short walk back to the workshop.

He sprang up onto the workbench.

"The moon is just about to catch the cockerel," he whispered to Mr Elvic, who smiled back.

"As I was saying," continued Mrs Gee. "I shall never shout at … oh my goodness me. What am I doing here at this time of the day? It must be time for my tea."

She looked slightly confused – the magic had gone.

"You just popped in for a short chat," said Mr Elvic.

"Was it about that cat?" she asked, pointing a finger at Benson.

She was just about to shout at Benson when she stopped and smiled.

"Well, I must go. I can't believe what the time is. I do feel a little light-headed. I must be hungry," she murmured.

"Don't forget your bike then," said Mr Elvic, pointing to the new one.

"That's not mine … is it?" said Mrs Gee, something stirring in her distant memory.

"Yes, it's yours. We thought you deserved it," replied Mr Elvic. "Now say no more about it."

Mrs Gee looked at the beautiful bike.

"It's like the bike in my dream," she whispered, "are you sure?"

"I'm sure," said Mr Elvic, the wrinkles by his eyes smiling.

Benson purred his loudest purr. The pink star on the bell caught Mrs Gee's eye and winked.

"Yes. It is my bike, don't ask me how, but it is," she said very quietly. "Thank you, Mr Elvic. Thank you, Benson."

She walked out of the workshop and rode her bike the wrong way up the one-way lane and home.

Mr Elvic and Benson looked at each other and smiled. Mr Elvic gently pulled the ginger cat's ears.

"That's one happy lady," said Benson, "what an adventure we've had. I am quite worn out."

Mr Elvic glanced at the alarm clock inside the wooden case of the old clock on the wall.

"Time I was on my way as well," he replied. "Are you going to finish that tin of tuna off while I move Mrs Gee's old bike? She didn't even give it one glance. I can use it for spares."

"Yes thanks, it's a while since I had that ice cream," said Benson, jumping down from the bench, and immediately tucking into the food.

Mr Elvic hung the old bike from a hook high up on the wall and then went around the workshop, switching off the gas heater and lights, and making sure the doors were locked. As they stepped out onto the pavement, Mr Elvic bent down and stroked Benson.

"We've had quite a day. Take care now, little chap, sleep tight,"

"'Bye, Mr E.," sighed Benson, watching his friend lock the door and get into his car. He waved his paw as the car went down the lane and disappeared round the corner. He looked across at the school and wondered sort of a day Rosie had had. Oh how he wanted to tell her about his adventure, but he knew he couldn't. Benson shivered. The night was getting chilly and it was time for him to stake his claim for the cosy armchair in the furniture-shop yard. He crept into the yard quietly, his ears up and alert, just in case Bubble, Squeak and Zimba were on the prowl.

It was all clear and Benson leapt up into the armchair and wriggled around until he was comfortable. His eyes began to close. He was sure he could hear Dowter the dog barking in the distance, asking to be let inside. As the moon looked down on him, Benson began to snore gently ... *and dreamed the dreams that only cats can dream*...

Though perhaps this time he dreamt of bikes!

10

BENSON GOES ON A CAR JOURNEY

Benson was enjoying his early-morning drink of milk when Bob arrived to do his usual sweeping up.

"Morning, Mr E.," he called, "how are you today?"

"I'm fine, Bob, and you?" enquired Mr Elvic.

"Just a few aches and pains," replied Bob, "nothing too bad."

"That's good, I'm glad," said Benson.

Bob blinked and peered closely at Mr Elvic.

"You said that without moving your lips," he said in amazement. "How did you do it?"

"It must have been a trick of the light," replied Mr Elvic, shooting a warning glance at Benson, who was now sitting by the stove. He flicked his ears backwards and forwards at Mr Elvic.

"It was that or I need my glasses changing," laughed Bob.

"I have to take a machine to Grimble Town Football Club this morning, so I'll leave you to sweep up and answer the phone if that's OK," explained Mr Elvic to Bob.

"That's fine. I can do that," replied Bob smiling. He

liked to be left in charge, it made him feel important. "I shall have to pop out for a few minutes though, because I'm having a new chair delivered."

"OK, I'll try not to be too long," said Mr Elvic, getting the car keys out of his overalls pocket. "Come on now, Benson, out you go for a while."

Benson opened his mouth, then remembered and shut it quickly. He didn't want to go outside, he had only just got warmed up. He looked at Mr Elvic pleadingly with his big green eyes.

"Benson! *Out you go*," said Mr Elvic, winking his eye at him. Benson reluctantly left the warm spot near the stove and slunk outside and sat near the car.

"Benson, Benson, yoo hoo," called a voice.

It was Rosie playing in the playground with her friends.

"That's my special friend, Benson," he heard her telling her friends.

"Oh yeah, and what's so special about a cat?" a little boy asked.

"Careful Rosie, careful," said Benson quietly to himself.

"He's soft and furry to touch, and he's so friendly," he heard Rosie reply.

Suddenly, two legs in blue overalls appeared in front of him. It was Mr Elvic.

"I would have behaved myself with Bob if you had let me stay in the warm," whispered Benson as Mr Elvic bent down to stroke him.

"I thought you might fancy a ride out in the car to the football club," his friend whispered back.

"Wowee," shouted Benson, he'd never been in a car before.

"Shush, you'll have Bob out here wondering what's going on," said Mr Elvic, chuckling and opening the back door. "Come on, quickly, in you get."

Benson didn't need telling twice. He sprang lightly up onto the soft grey material of the back seat. He watched out of the back window as Mr Elvic hung the trailer onto the tow bar of the car, with the machine for the football club tightly tied to it.

Mr Elvic climbed into the driver's seat, closed the door and put on his seat belt. Benson watched as all the dials lit up on the dashboard and needles swung round as Mr Elvic turned the key in the ignition and started the car's engine. The car began to vibrate gently as the engine warmed up. Then Mr Elvic wiggled his feet around on pedals near the floor, and moved a thing that, to Benson, looked like a stick. Benson felt the car move. His fur stood on end with excitement as Mr Elvic drove the car out into the lane, making it turn in the right direction with a big wheel he was holding in his hands.

Benson looked out of the back window to see Mrs Gee approaching on her new bike, waving to people as if she were the Queen!

"Mrs Gee is coming," he warned Mr Elvic.

"Yes, I've seen her. I'll let her come past," replied Mr Elvic, "it might be safer. I don't want her to land in the back of the trailer."

He stopped the car and waited for the vision in pink to ride by.

Benson noticed Rosie waving to him from the

playground, so he waved his paw back, just as Mrs Gee came riding stately by on her new bike.

"Good heavens, that Benson is waving to someone," she cried as she went past, "whatever next?"

Mrs Gee turned back to look at Benson again.

"Oh no," said Mr Elvic, "look!"

A furniture van was parked outside Bob's delivering his new chair. The ramp of the van was down, and Bob was just coming out of the workshop to let the delivery men in to his house.

Mrs Gee shot up the ramp of the van making the two delivery men leap for their lives. The bike came to a halt when it collided with Bob's chair, but Mrs Gee carried on. She somersaulted through the air as if she had been shot out of a cannon and landed on a settee at the other end of the van. For a few seconds all was silent, then a podgy hand appeared and the furniture rattled and shook as Mrs Gee pulled herself to her feet. Her head appeared above the chair, her pink furry hat all to one side, and her round face all red and flustered.

"My bike, my beautiful bike, is it all right?" she cried.

"Never mind your bike, what about my chair?" shouted Bob. "It's taken me ages to save up for that. Why can't you be more careful?"

"It wasn't my fault. That cat was waving to someone," cried Mrs Gee, two tears running down her fat cheeks.

"Oh don't talk rubbish, cats can't wave," said Bob, rushing to inspect has chair.

"But..." Mrs Gee gave up. "Bob, I'm so sorry. Is my bike all right?" she asked.

"I'm sorry for shouting at you," said Bob. "Let's have a look."

He helped the quivering lady from the furniture van just as the two delivery men appeared from its side.

"Is it safe to come back in?" one of them asked.

"I think so," said Bob. "Help me to sort this chair and bike out, please."

The men helped to lift the chair and bike out of the van, and they all had a good look at them.

"Not a mark or scratch on anything," declared Bob, "no harm done, except for you giving yourself a fright, Mrs Gee. What a smart bike! Is it new?"

"Yes, very new," said Mrs Gee, looking proudly at the winking pink star on the bell. "Let's see if I can ride into town without any more mishaps," she continued as she got onto her bike again. "'Bye, Bob, see you later."

"I'm sure that cat was waving," she said under her breath. "Still, I don't know why, but I can't be cross with him. I suppose I must have looked rather funny, flying through the air like that."

Mrs Gee began to laugh at herself. Louder and louder she shrieked passing astonished looking shoppers on the way.

"We must be on our way. Everyone seems to be OK," chuckled Mr Elvic to Benson.

Bob was showing the delivery men where the chair was to go, and then he would go back to the workshop.

Mr Elvic passed the furniture van with care, and signalled to turn left at the bottom of the lane.

Benson could hear the tick, tick, tick of the indicators. It reminded him of the clock in the workshop. He usually went to sleep listening to the ticking, but not today, oh no, he was being taken on a journey out into an exciting world that he had never seen before. Up to now, Benson's world had been around Cinder Lane. He had lived with kind old Mrs Tutts until she died a few weeks ago. He had really missed her and nobody seemed to want to look after him, so he managed to do that for himself. Then he had met Mr Elvic and his life had changed completely. He sat on the back seat of the car as it made its way into town. His wide green eyes were trying to take in every new sight.

They turned right past the hairdresser's; Benson could see ladies with funny looking machines on their heads, sitting in a row looking at magazines. They went past the pizza house, tobacconist, and Chinese takeaway. Benson's nose began to twitch – there was a familiar smell. The beautiful smell of fish.

"There's 'The Plaice' where I get the fish and chips from," pointed out Mr Elvic.

Benson's mouth was watering at the very thought of all that fish in one place. When they reached the corner, Benson could see people sitting at tables inside the Wheatsheaf public house. He could just see a flicker of the fire through the window – it all looked very friendly and cosy.

Benson sat transfixed as they turned into the main street of the town. To him there seemed to be people everywhere, going about their business.

"This isn't busy," said Mr Elvic, "you should see it on market day."

Benson could see the rows of cream cakes as they passed the bakery. He knew what they were because Mrs Tutts used to have one as a treat.

Rows of shining rings in trays caught his eyes, glinting under bright lights in the jewellery shop.

"There's the market square," pointed out Mr Elvic. "On market days stall holders come and sell flowers, fruit, slippers, vegetables, cheese and lots of other things from stalls outside."

Benson looked across to the square. He could see a few people sitting on seats around the square – some reading newspapers, others just sitting and talking to each other. He gazed at this new world opening up all around him. They passed the butcher's shop with the portly butchers in their bright-white coats and hats. They passed the newsagent's, with its shelves full of newspapers and magazines.

"That's where I go to have my eyes tested and get my glasses," said Mr Elvic.

Benson looked at the optician's window full of glasses looking back at him – black frames, silver, gold, red and many more colours, catching the light shining on them.

They rounded the corner towards the church. The traffic lights near the church were on red, so the traffic was at a standstill.

"Wow!" exclaimed Benson, "I didn't realise just how tall the church spire was."

He twisted and turned his neck, trying to get the best view of the beautiful church and its spectacular spire out of the window. In the end he lay down on his back on the seat, four paws waving in the air. From there he got a super view of the church, looking up its towering spire right up to the cockerel at the very top.

"I can see the cockerel that the moon catches," he shouted excitedly to Mr Elvic.

They moved through the traffic lights, and Benson sat up and looked at the church from the back window.

"Get out of sight quickly," said Mr Elvic, "it's Mrs Gee. She must be doing a tour of the town on her new bike."

Benson crouched down. Mrs Gee sailed by in stately fashion, waving and ringing her bell as she saw Mr Elvic in his car.

"I'm not looking back this time," she said to herself, "that cat might be waving at me again!"

She giggled, thinking about the events of earlier. She had had a wonderful time riding around Lud and showing off her new bike.

Over the bridge they went, passing the old water mill. Benson caught a brief glimpse of the river, rippling and bubbling on its way, shaded by trees, some of which were overhanging the water.

"Can you see the white house halfway up the hill?" asked Mr Elvic.

"Yes, just," replied Benson.

"That's where Mrs E.'s sister lives. The garden is lovely and it goes right down to the riverbank. The bungalow opposite the white house is where her brother lives with his wife," explained Mr Elvic.

94

By now they were picking up speed and heading out towards the country – round the big roundabout with the tractor company near by, blue and red tractors on display behind the huge glass windows. Benson was having the time of his life trying to take in all the sights.

"What are all those rabbits doing out of their cages?" he asked in amazement as they passed a family of rabbits playing in a field not far from the road. "Isn't it dangerous for them?"

"They are wild rabbits that live in the countryside and look after themselves. They are usually just brown in colour," explained Mr Elvic, enjoying having someone to talk to. He usually made these journeys alone, except for the odd times when Mrs Elvic accompanied him. A huge lorry with a row of lights on top of the cab rumbled by, surprising Benson.

"Gosh! That lorry was even bigger than the bin lorries that drive down the lane," exclaimed the happy, curious cat.

Mr Elvic smiled to himself. He knew that there was a field of cows round the next corner – what would Benson make of those?

"Oh wow! What are those?" cried Benson as the black-and-white creatures came into sight.

"They are cows and they give us milk," said Mr Elvic.

"Milk? The milkman brings your milk," exclaimed Benson.

"Yes, that's right, but the cows are milked in a dairy, and then the milk is put into bottles for the milkman to deliver," explained Mr Elvic.

"Then I drink it as belly fodder!" said Benson.

"I suppose you could say that," chuckled Mr Elvic, pulling over and stopping the car in a lay-by near the field. "Let's take a closer look at them."

"I don't know if I want to," came the nervous reply.

"They won't hurt you, little chap," Mr Elvic said, getting out of the car. He came round and opened the back door. Benson timidly crept out of the car and stayed close to his friend. Mr Elvic leant his arms on the fence, and Benson peered through it at the big sturdy creatures Mr Elvic called "cows". The three nearest ones to the fence stopped munching the grass and stared directly at the two friends. Their large doleful eyes looked intently at Mr Elvic and Benson. Puffs of breath could be seen in the winter air as they blew and flared their nostrils. One of the cows decided to amble closer to the fence. Benson hid behind Mr Elvic's legs. Closer and closer it came.

"Let's get back in the car," said Benson in a tiny voice.

To Benson the cow looked like a huge black-and-white monster bearing down on them. He was sure it could jump the fence. Mr Elvic scooped the frightened cat up into his arms.

"Look, it's quite friendly," he said, stroking the cow's nose.

"Be careful, Mr E., be careful," whined Benson, shaking.

"Just keep calm – I won't let it hurt you," soothed Mr Elvic.

Without warning the cow put back its head and mooed.

"Aaargh!" yelled Benson.

"MOOO!" replied the cow.

"Ooooo ah!" cried Benson, scrambling up out of Mr Elvic's arms, over his shoulder and down onto the ground.

"Mooo," went the cow again.

That was quite enough for Benson, and he took a flying leap and landed on the roof of the car in a heap, panting for breath, his paws covering his eyes.

"I knew it was a monster," he cried, "come away, Mr E., please, come away."

Nobody answered him.

"It's taken him away. I'll never see him again. How am I going to get back to Cinder Lane?" thought the cat, his imagination running riot.

As he lay there with his paws still over his eyes, he could hear the drone of the traffic going past.

"Perhaps someone will stop and help me," he thought.

Suddenly, he felt a caring hand touch him. He knew that touch! His heart leapt and he cautiously opened one eye. There were a pair of glasses, with gentle grey eyes, looking at him over the roof of the car.

"Mr E.," cried the cat. "You are still here!" and he rolled across the roof of the car and landed with his paws around Mr Elvic's neck, hugging him as best as a cat *can* hug.

"There is no need to be frightened. The cow was only talking in cow talk. Look in the field now," encouraged Mr Elvic.

Benson peeped up from Mr Elvic's safe shoulders

and looked at the field with amazement. All of the cows were calmly munching the grass.

"I do feel daft, but it really did make me jump," he said.

"It was rather a loud moo, I must admit. Come along now, we must continue our journey," said Mr Elvic, opening the car door.

Benson jumped in and thankfully sank down on the soft seat. They travelled through several small villages. Benson looked at the houses and cottages clustered around the village greens. He caught sight of grey churches with towers, small shops by the roadside and trees – he had never seen so many tall trees. Some were long and thin, and others had huge thick branches that spread-eagled in all directions. He spotted a tractor working in a brown field with big white birds following it.

Eventually, the fields disappeared and they were driving down long, and much busier, roads and streets, with long rows of houses on either side. Mr Elvic stopped and started several times as they came up to roundabouts, traffic lights and road junctions.

"Here we are," said Mr Elvic, turning the car down a narrow side street, and pulling into a bumpy car park. "Here's the football club where Mrs E. and the family come to watch football matches."

"What happens in a football match?" asked Benson, wanting to learn as much as possible.

Mr Elvic rubbed his chin.

"Well, there are two teams of eleven people, and they kick a football around – you know what a ball is?" Benson nodded. "They have to see which team can score most goals. A goal is when the ball goes between two poles at the end of a field, without cows, and the poles have a bar across the top. Whichever team scores the most goals wins the match."

Benson wasn't too sure if he understood what it was really all about – no doubt it would become clearer.

"Hello, hello," boomed a voice.

"Hi there, Charlie," shouted Mr Elvic, winding down the window.

"I'll just open the big gates, then you can reverse in, and we can unload the machine," boomed Charlie again. Charlie was the man who looked after the grass at the football club along with some other helpers.

Benson watched Charlie unlock the massive gates. He had red overalls on (much like Mr Elvic's blue ones) and long black wellington boots (not a bit like Mrs Gee's). He looked at the tall, long buildings of the football club, towering over the row of small terraced houses near by, making them look like dolls' houses. The gates were opened and Mr Elvic started slowly reversing through them. Charlie was waving his hands about, helping to direct them through safely. Benson stifled a laugh. Charlie really did look funny, and he was sure that Mr Elvic wasn't taking the slightest bit of notice of him. The car came to a standstill.

"You had better stay in the car out of harm's way," Mr Elvic said quietly.

Before Benson could answer, the car door was pulled open.

"Hello, hello," boomed Charlie again. His face matched the red of his overalls, and his eyes were of the brightest blue you could ever see. He patted Mr Elvic on the shoulder with one of the biggest hands Benson had ever seen.

"Good of you to come today. I know how busy you are. Goodness me, is that a cat on the seat? Well, I never! Now then, how's Mrs E. and those two granddaughters of yours?" chattered Charlie.

Mr Elvic kept opening his mouth but couldn't get a word in. Charlie continued to wave his arms around excitedly, a smile lighting up his ruddy face. Mr Elvic got out of the car, and he and Charlie set about unloading the machine from the trailer. Benson looked around him. So this was Grimble Town Football Club. He gazed round at the four big stands that made up the sides of the ground. There were rows and rows of seats – black, white and red. He wondered where Mrs Elvic and the family sat, and he tried to imagine all the seats full of people, and the noise they would make. He didn't think he would like it because he wasn't keen on loud noise! He supposed the loudest noise would be the cheer when the players scored a goal. He spotted the white posts Mr Elvic had mentioned, the nets hanging between them like giant cobwebs at either end of the pitch. One of Charlie's helpers came slowly by the car, pushing a machine along, marking the white lines on the football pitch. The machine looked like a box on wheels with long handles fastened to it. Benson watched fascinated as the white line appeared from the bottom of it, and he sprang onto the driver's seat to get a better look at it.

"That's like magic," he murmured. Benson liked magic!

"Tom! Tom," boomed a voice, "time for coffee."

Tom stopped pushing the machine and disappeared into the groundsman's hut to have a coffee with Charlie and Mr Elvic. Benson looked at the machine and glanced around. No one was about; dare he go and look at that machine? He poked his head out of the open window. He fancied some fresh air – surely a little wander wouldn't do any harm. Lightly and swiftly he jumped down onto the ground, and put a paw onto the green grass. It felt lovely to touch – so soft to his paws, just like a green carpet. Benson grew more and more confident and walked right onto the pitch and towards the white-line machine. He stopped when he reached it, sniffed and craned his neck to look inside the metal box on wheels. He could just see some white liquid inside it.

"Mmm, that looks like cream," he thought, "I'll take a closer look."

He scrambled up and balanced on the thin edge of the box and leant forward to sniff at it again. He gave a big sniff this time.

"Phew! That's not cream. It's like smelly cabbage in a dustbin."

The smell got right up Benson's nose and it made him want to sneeze. His nose began to twitch and tingle. He lifted a paw to rub his nose and he began to wobble. His ears flicked backwards and forwards, and his tail waved frantically in the air.

"*Aaaaa-TISHOOO*!" came the explosion, followed by a splash of white liquid. Benson had fallen in!

"Oops! What have I done?" came a startled voice from the box.

Benson was white from his neck to the tip of his ginger tail.

"I think I had better get out of here," he said to himself, and he scrambled up and out of the box, and stood in an ever-growing puddle of white liquid.

"Whatever am I going to do? I can't lick myself clean," wondered Benson, "and I'm going to be in bother if Mr E. sees me like this. Whatever will Charlie say?"

He frantically looked around – nobody was in sight. There was a sprinkler watering the grass at the other side of the pitch and that was all. SPRINKLER?

"That's the only chance I'll have to clean myself up," the worried cat thought, and he ran across the pitch towards the sprinkler. He left a neat line of white paw prints all the way across the pitch! Benson glanced nervously around when he reached the sprinkler, and realised that this was going to be cold!

"It's now or never, boy – go for it!"

Benson ran under the fountain of water and squawked.

"Oooooh, this is freezing," he said, and began to jump up and down on all four paws, leaving splashes of white all over the pitch near the sprinkler.

"It's just like heavy rain," thought Benson, beginning to enjoy himself. He started to dance and skip around under the mushroom of water. Round and round he scampered, jumping, forwards and backwards, round and round, chasing his own tail.

"I feel a song coming on," he cried, flinging his head in the air and water flying everywhere.

> *"Water Machine, Water Machine,*
> *Will you please make me clean?*
> *I didn't mean to get all white*
> *I gave myself a real big fright,"*

Benson sang at the top of his voice.

"There, that's got all the white out of my fur," he continued, giving one last spring into the sprinkling water. "Now I must get dry somehow. I know. I'll do what the footballers do and run up and down the pitch. I'll pretend I'm playing football."

He ran to the centre circle, stood still for a second and then he was off – running here and there, dipping and dodging, pretending he was kicking the football past all the other players.

"I'm going for goal," he cried, "yeeess! I've scored."

He spun round in the goal mouth and ran all the way back up the pitch to where Mr Elvic had left the car. What he didn't know was that he had left a trail of white paw prints all over the pitch – the underneath of his paws were still white! Oh dear!

A few minutes later, he heard Mr Elvic say, "Thanks for the coffee, Charlie, I'll be on my way now. I hope the machine will be OK now."

Mr Elvic got into the car.

"Are you having a catnap, Benson?" he asked, looking at the ginger cat curled up in a fluffy ball on the back seat. Benson pretended to snore.

As they drove through the gates he heard a voice boom out.

"Tom, what have you been doing?" roared Charlie. "Look at this mess!"

"Oh dear, whatever is the matter with Charlie?" said Mr Elvic, looking in his car mirror.

In the reflection he could see Charlie standing on the pitch, hands on hips, shaking his head in disbelief. Poor Tom was standing, arms outstretched, and shrugging his shoulders. Benson snored on and *dreamed the dreams that only cats can dream…*

11

IVAN REVEALS HIS WISH

Mr Elvic was standing in the queue at "The Plaice", waiting to buy lunch for Benson and himself. Ivan, the young decorator, was standing in front of him looking very serious and sad.

"You're very quiet, Ivan, are you all right?" enquired Mr Elvic.

"No, I'm not all right, I am very upset," Ivan replied, looking desolate.

"Whatever is the matter?" asked Mr Elvic, sounding concerned.

"You know I was decorating at Woodhills Retirement Home?" Mr Elvic nodded. "Well, I had just about finished when a water pipe burst and ruined all my work – not to mention some of the carpets. Dr Doit has had to move all six elderly people to different homes while it is all sorted out. They are all so upset at having to live apart," explained Ivan, looking as if he was about to cry.

"Oh dear, I'm so sorry," replied Mr Elvic sympathetically. "Is there anything I can do?"

"I don't think so," said Ivan, "but thanks anyway. I

just wish that I could wave a wand and summon up some magic helpers from somewhere to get the job done in the wink of an eye … but that's just wishful thinking. By the way, my big ladder needs mending. I'll pop it in this afternoon for you to look at."

Mr Elvic's heart began to beat faster and faster, and thoughts raced through his mind. It was Wednesday – the "wish-day"! Could he use the Wishing Machine to help Ivan, Dr Doit and the residents of Woodhills? He couldn't get served quickly enough and rushed back to talk to Benson. He narrowly missed getting knocked over by Mrs Gee careering round the corner on her bike.

"Hello, Mr Elvic," she shrilled.

He flew in through the workshop door, waking Benson from a sweet dream about the biggest fish, the best belly fodder, he had ever seen!

"Good gracious, what's the matter with you?" the cat exclaimed. "For goodness sake sit down before you fall down. Has someone been chasing you?"

"No, no, nothing like that," puffed Mr Elvic, sitting in his swivel chair in the office. Benson ran after him, wondering what had happened. As they ate their fish and chips, Mr Elvic explained all about Woodhills, while Benson listened with great interest – his ears going backwards and forwards.

"We must try to help them," exclaimed Benson when Mr Elvic had finished the sad tale, "Dr. Doit will be most upset."

"Ivan did wish that he could wave a wand and summon up some magic helpers," said Mr Elvic, his eyes shining with anticipation, "I thought we could use the Wishing Machine again, it is the wish-day."

"How would we get the star into Ivan's hand?" questioned Benson.

"That's just it. His big ladder needs mending and he is bringing it here this afternoon for me to have a look at," said Mr Elvic, swivelling excitedly round in his chair, grabbing the keys to the back door.

"We've no time to lose then," said Benson. "Let me just finish my belly fodder."

He gobbled down the last few flakes of his fish, wiped his whiskers clean with his paws, and scampered round the machines, arriving at the back door as Mr Elvic unlocked it. They scurried down the steps into the courtyard and to the door of the Rainstar Palace. Mr Elvic's hands were shaking as he put the key in upside down, turned it three times to the right, twice to the left and pushed the door.

"It won't open," he cried, pushing again.

"How about knocking twice on the knob?" Benson reminded him.

"Phew, thanks, little chap, I'm getting carried away."

Mr Elvic knocked twice on the knob and the door slowly creaked open. Benson tingled with excitement from the tip of his nose to the end of his tail. Once again the two friends entered the darkness of the Rainstar Palace, and a few stars on the cover lit up as if to welcome them. The large, nosy spider swung down out of his web, cross at being disturbed.

For a few seconds the web looked as if it had been painted, as the colours of the stars caught it. Mr Elvic took the cover off the Wishing Machine.

They had to be as quick as they possibly could be today, because there was no telling what time Ivan would arrive with his ladder.

They stepped up to the timeless machine. Benson didn't need telling what to do – he placed his paw on the handle and waited. He heard the click of the machine being switched on, and felt Mr Elvic hold his tail. The machine whirred into life, louder and louder, and then … silence. The bright red glow spread through the machine, becoming brighter and brighter, lighting the room like a furnace. Then it was gone and stars shot rapidly through the machine. It was as if someone had lifted the lid off a treasure trove and found hundreds of glittering jewels.

"Wish, wish, wish, wish …" came the haunting voice, its whispers filling the room.

Mr Elvic cleared his throat.

"Ah-um, I would like to make a wish for Ivan the painter and decorator. He wished for a wand to summon up magic helpers to help him put right all the damage the burst water pipes have done at Woodhills Retirement Home."

Benson gasped as the tingling sensation warmed the whole of his body, right to the tip of his tail. Once again, he and Mr Elvic were joined by a rope of vibrant light as the stars raced through their bodies.

"Your wish is granted," came the whisper. "Don't forget to catch a star, and look out for a silver wand in the tunnel of colour."

"I hope we have better luck this time. We nearly didn't catch a star for Mrs Gee," thought Benson, as he watched the stars flicker and fade away.

They both let go of the Wishing Machine. A smiling Mr Elvic turned to Benson.

"That's the easy part done, now for the tricky bit. Are you ready?"

Benson nodded, getting ready to spring. Mr Elvic took hold of the corners of the star-filled cover and shook it. Hundreds of stars flew off it, twinkling and sparkling, cascading down like a fountain lit up at night. Benson gazed, mesmerised by the beautiful sight.

"Benson, try and catch a star, instead of standing there gawping," shouted Mr Elvic. Benson came back to earth with a jolt. He opened his mouth to say sorry when he felt something fluttering in the roof of it.

"Whatever is that?" wondered Benson.

Then it fluttered over his tongue! Benson realised it was a star and shut his mouth quickly, trying not to swallow. Mr Elvic was jumping here and there, arms twirling all over the place.

"BENSON! WILL YOU HELP?" he shouted, between desperate lunges at the darting stars, which were quickly beginning to settle down on the blue velvet cover.

Benson could not move. If he opened his mouth the star would fly out, and what's more, it was beginning to tickle him and make him giggle. Mr Elvic made a last dive as the last star landed. Puffing and red in the face, he looked at Benson.

"Well, you were really helpful there. What is the matter with you?" he gasped.

Benson could not answer his friend, but kept on giggling as the star tickled his mouth.

"It's all right you laughing Benson, it's not at all funny," said Mr Elvic, glaring at Benson through the gloom.

"Are you ignoring me on purpose?" he asked, when Benson did not speak.

He bent down to take a closer look at the cat. Tears of cat laughter were rolling down Benson's ginger cheeks – but still he kept his mouth shut. He pointed to a star on the cover and then pointed to his mouth.

"You've caught a star in your mouth? You clever cat, I'm most impressed," exclaimed Mr Elvic.

He whipped his bobble hat off his head, and put it over Benson's mouth.

Benson opened his mouth. "Ha, ha, ha, ha," he laughed and blew the star into the waiting hat.

"Have you caught it?" he cried through the tears of laughter.

"Yes. It's a silver one this time," replied Mr Elvic, carefully placing the hat back safely on his head. "I am sorry I shouted at you, but I didn't realise what had happened."

He gently pulled Benson's ears and chuckled along with his friend.

"We should get back to the workshop and wait for Ivan to arrive," he continued, covering the Wishing Machine.

As they reached the door, Benson turned and quietly said, "Goodbye for now, you wonderful Wishing Machine."

A red star winked. And then all was quiet. All was still.

12

THE DYLINGS DO THE DECORATING

Benson was snoozing by the wood stove, and Mr Elvic was standing tinkering with a lawnmower that was on the bench in front of him. He glanced up and caught sight of the top of Ivan's ladder going past the window.

"He's here, Benson," he said urgently, "get ready."

Mr Elvic retrieved the silver star from his bobble hat and waited for the door to open. Benson wandered over and sat close to him. In came Ivan, dressed in his dungarees and a red jumper that clashed with his short ginger hair. Freckles covered his young face.

"Hi there, Ivan," Mr Elvic greeted him cheerfully.

"Hello there, where shall I put the ladder?" asked Ivan, sounding miserable.

"Just lean it against the wall where you are," replied Mr Elvic, smiling broadly, "then come over here – I've something to show you."

Ivan placed the ladder against the wall and walked over to Mr Elvic, looking puzzled.

"What is it?" enquired Ivan, "I could do with a good laugh."

"Hold out your hand, palm upwards," said Mr Elvic, his eyes twinkling mischievously.

"I don't know whether I should," said the young decorator nervously, "are you playing a trick on me?"

"Do as I ask and then you will see," said Mr Elvic, winking at Benson.

Slowly, Ivan stretched out his hand towards Mr Elvic. The silver star was quickly pressed into the palm of his hand, and for a moment they both froze like statues.

Benson watched, wide-eyed, as a silver glow formed around them, glistening like Jack Frost on a cold, crisp, winter's morning. Suddenly, their hands parted and Benson leapt into Mr Elvic's arms – he knew what was coming.

Ivan looked first at Benson, and then at Mr Elvic.

"What's happening?" he mouthed, no sound coming out, his ginger hair standing on end.

He gasped in amazement as a stream of brilliant stars flew from the silver one in his palm, his mouth opening and closing like a goldfish's (and like Mrs Gee's!). Soon the workshop was full of stars of every colour, floating about as if a bag of glitter had been emptied from the roof.

"It's all right, Ivan, don't be afraid," Benson just managed to shout before the vivid, colourful tunnel began to form, swirling all around them.

"I must be dreaming – that cat spoke … wwwhhoooo," cried Ivan, as all three went tumbling through the tunnel of colour.

Benson leapt from Mr Elvic's arms and squealed, "I'm flying," and stretched all four legs out like aeroplane wings, his tail streaming out behind him. On and on they tumbled, Benson turning this way and that, flapping his legs wide like birds' wings.

"What's happening?" cried Ivan again, as he somersaulted passed Mr Elvic.

Mr Elvic suddenly remembered that they had to look out for a silver wand in the tunnel – he hoped that they had not missed it.

"Look out for a silver wand coming and grab it if you see it," he shouted, doing his own somersault to catch up with Ivan.

"What do you want a wand for?" asked the astonished young man, floating alongside Mr Elvic.

"You wished for one to summon magic helpers to help you sort out Woodhills Home for the elderly residents," replied Mr Elvic.

"That would be wonderful. What an amazing dream I'm having," said Ivan, shaking his head.

Mr Elvic suddenly noticed the silver wand floating towards them.

"Ivan! The wand! It's coming! Catch it!" he shouted.

Ivan stretched out his arm and caught the wand safely in his hand.

The tunnel of light began to fade, they all slowed down and the light disappeared. Gently, they landed in a garden. There was a splash followed by a yowl of horror. Benson had not been watching what he was doing and had landed in the pond.

"Trust you, Benson!" said Mr Elvic, laughing and helping the bedraggled cat out of the pond, knocking a lily pad off his head and pulling weed out of his ears.

Benson gave himself a shake – he felt silly.

"Does anyone know where we are?" he asked, standing in a puddle of pond water.

"Wait a minute. I recognise this garden – we are at Woodhills Retirement Home!" cried Ivan. "Wow, what a way to arrive here. I usually drive here in my van. If we follow the gravel path between the tall hedge and the weeping willow trees, we shall come to the house."

"You lead the way then, and let's hope Benson dries out on the way," said Mr Elvic. "And don't lose the wand!" he added.

"I hope I dry out. That wind is a bit nippy today, and I don't want frostbite in my tail," replied Benson.

They crunched along the narrow gravel path, past the graceful willow trees, whose branches seemed to be waving "hello" in the stiff winter breeze. Keeping close to the tall hedge they rounded the corner and the house came into view.

It was a beautiful, big, old house built from red bricks. Tall chimneys rose up from the roof, and there were long oblong windows upstairs and downstairs – all painted white. The gravel path widened out into a sweeping drive in the front of the house. A ramp led up to the huge, black front door with a gold bell to press.

"Do you think anyone is at home?" asked Ivan nervously. "They are going to wonder what we are doing here."

"Don't worry, Ivan, it's magic," Mr Elvic assured him as he pressed the bell.

"I know, but I am still confused as to what is going on," replied Ivan.

Mr Elvic was about to explain to Ivan when the door swung slowly open, as if to beckon them in.

"Ooooh, who opened that? There's nobody there!" said Ivan, shivering.

"Come along, I'm sure it's all right," said Mr Elvic, "let's go inside."

"You go in first, and I'll follow," whispered Ivan, his teeth chattering and his heart thumping.

Mr Elvic and Benson walked into the large airy entrance hall, over the WELCOME door mat and onto the white-and-black tiles that covered the floor. The walls were white with a hint of pink in the paint, and a vase of lovely yellow roses stood on a small polished table.

"Hello. Anyone here?" shouted Mr Elvic.

No one replied.

"There's nobody here – come in, Ivan," called Benson.

The decorator's ginger head appeared round the door as he nervously walked in clutching the wand.

"Where is the room that's damaged?" asked Mr Elvic.

"Follow me and I'll show you," replied Ivan, feeling more confident.

He led them through a door, down a long corridor and into the spacious room that was the lounge.

"This is the room where they gather to watch the

telly, play bingo, have a chat and lots more besides," explained Ivan, "but just look at it now."

"What a mess!" sighed Mr Elvic, looking up at the ceiling hanging down in parts, and the wallpaper sadly drooping on the walls.

"They had to take the lovely chandelier light down because the water had ruined all the wires, and take up the soft red carpet and throw it away," said Ivan sadly.

"Such a lot of work needs doing. We shall certainly need help, that's for sure," exclaimed Mr Elvic. "Time to summon up those magic helpers, Ivan"

"But what do I do?" said Ivan, looking at the wand.

"Well, try waving the wand around and asking for help," suggested Benson.

"I shall feel so silly," said Ivan, his face turning bright red. "Oh well, it's only a dream – here goes."

He lifted his arm and waved the wand in the air.

"Please could I summon some magic helpers to make everything right again?" he called, his voice echoing round the empty room.

All three of them stood quietly and very still. They could hear the birds twittering outside and the breeze blowing branches against a window somewhere.

Nothing happened.

"Try again," said Mr Elvic quietly.

Ivan waved the wand and asked for help again. They waited … nothing!

"It's not working," Ivan said helplessly, "it's hopeless!"

"No, it's not! Be patient, we mustn't give up. We

can't let Dr. Doit and his friends down," exclaimed Mr Elvic, his eyes travelling around the big room.

"Oh, there's the old teapot in the corner – the one that they are always breaking."

Catching his eye, something silver winked at Mr Elvic.

"The workmen used the teapot when they came to take up the carpet," explained Ivan.

Mr Elvic blinked and looked at the teapot – there it was again – a silver wink, this time brighter. Brighter and brighter the tiny silver light became and winked faster and faster. Mr Elvic couldn't tear his eyes away. Wondering what their friend was looking at, Benson and Ivan followed his gaze to the teapot, and then it was their turn to be mesmerised by the flashing light. Then it stopped!

"Whatever was that?" stuttered Ivan.

Mr Elvic walked across to the teapot, picked it up and brought it back to Benson and Ivan.

"Look at this," he whispered excitedly.

They looked down and saw nestled in the centre of the teapot lid a silver star! As they looked, the star began to flicker and shine again.

"That's it," shouted Benson, "that star will some-how summon the magic helpers."

"Wowee!" cried Ivan, "but what do I do now?"

"Perhaps you need to touch the star with your silver wand," suggested Mr Elvic. "Maybe you could make up a rhyme as well. Let's all have a think."

The three friends all began to think of a rhyme. Benson's ears flicked backwards and forwards, Mr Elvic for once had a frown on his face, and Ivan's freckles seemed to be getting bigger. They stood in silence, their minds ticking over for ideas and inspiration. Mr Elvic shook his head.

"No. I can't think of anything," he said, looking very serious.

"Me neither … sorry," muttered Benson.

"Wait a minute, wait a minute, I think I've got it," cried Ivan, making Benson and Mr Elvic jump, "just give me a minute."

Ivan's face was a picture of concentration. He closed his eyes tightly and put his hands over his ears.

"Yes, I've got it," he spluttered.

He opened his eyes – bright shining eyes, full of hope. He pulled the silver wand from his big, deep decorator's pocket where he had put it for safe keeping. Touching the silver star with the tip of the wand, he began to speak in a clear and confident voice:

"Silver star, silver star,
Send me help from afar,
To make this room shine bright once more –
The damaged ceiling, walls and floor."

Not moving a muscle, Mr Elvic and Benson looked on in anticipation, their eyes firmly fixed on the teapot. Without warning, the teapot began to rattle and bounce up and down, and suddenly started taking great leaps around the floor, making the three friends scatter in all directions.

"Yikes!" yelled Ivan, diving to the floor as the

teapot leap-frogged over him, "that was a close call."

"Oooh, Mr E. I don't like this," cried Benson, his ginger fur standing on end. "Oooh, here it comes again."

The flying teapot bounced towards Benson, who took an almighty leap in the direction of Mr Elvic.

"Woooh – look out, Benson," shouted Mr Elvic, frantically trying to catch the cat in his out-stretched arms. Benson landed on Mr Elvic with a thump, knocking him off balance. Mr Elvic found himself running backwards, clutching the trembling cat.

"Look out – stop," he heard a voice cry.

Too late! Mr Elvic tripped over Ivan, who was still lying on the floor. For a few seconds they lay in a tangled heap on the dusty floorboards. Benson opened one green eye and cautiously looked around to locate the teapot. Ivan and Mr Elvic heard him gasp with amazement and scramble to his paws. Slowly they untangled themselves and clambered to their feet. Ivan's white dungarees were covered in dust. Mr Elvic straightened his hat and wiped his glasses clean.

"Just look at the teapot now," whispered Benson, pointing with his paw.

Sitting in the middle of the floor, the teapot was shining a brilliant silver colour, lighting up the room as if it was under floodlights at a football match. Then the light was gone!

Whoosh … a silver stream of steam rushed from the spout, quickly followed by a shower of sparkling silver stars that burst around the room like a firework lighting up the darkest night.

"What a beautiful sight!" exclaimed Ivan, his eyes shining in wonder.

A thin stream of silver steam began to trickle from the spout, gradually becoming stronger, until it was hissing like an angry dragon's nostril. Ivan stepped back, and Benson hid behind Mr Elvic's legs, only his shivering tail sticking out.

A shape began to form out of the silver steam – first, a large round head, followed by an equally large body. Mr Elvic took off his glasses and rubbed his eyes. Goodness gracious, was he seeing things? Benson dared to peep out from behind Mr Elvic and, with a pounding heart, watched in astonishment. By this time, Ivan was flat against the wall, eyes bulging, mouth wide open, trying to tell himself it was all a dream.

Two chubby arms appeared and a face formed, with two oval-shaped eyes, a squashed-looking nose and a large smiley mouth. There were no legs – just a short wispy tail.

Whatever it was wore a glittering silver waistcoat, and a white turban on its head, with one large silver star in the muddle of it. Clutched in one hand was a trumpet!

"Thank goodness for that," the vision suddenly said, "we've been stuck in there for years."

Benson leapt into Mr Elvic's arms in fright.

"It talks!" he stuttered.

"Of course I can talk," the vision replied, floating over to Mr Elvic and Benson. "Thank you for making a wish and asking us for help. Which one of you did it?"

"Tha-tha-that was mm-mm-me," Ivan stammered, very red in the face.

"Don't be frightened. I am Gawster, the master of the Dylings who are going to help you. I must call upon the others to appear, please excuse me."

Gawster floated over to the teapot, put the trumpet to his lips and began to play a lively, jazzy tune. Silver steam again began to ooze from the teapot's spout, and gradually another being began to form exactly the same as before. This Dyling had two silver stars in the middle of his turban and was carrying a trombone. Immediately the second Dyling was formed, he put the trombone to its lips and began to play alongside his friend. It was such a lively, catchy tune that Ivan and Mr Elvic couldn't help but click their fingers and sway to its rhythm. Benson twitched his ears backwards and forwards in time to the music. They watched as a third Dyling appeared, this time with three stars on his turban and carrying a silver clarinet, which he began to play. By this time, Ivan and Mr Elvic were clapping their hands together, and jiggling their legs about to the music. Not to be left out, Benson was making his tail go round in circles. Eventually the Dylings stopped playing and floated over.

"That was brilliant – it's ages since we have been able to make music," explained Gawster. "Let me introduce my brothers. This is Gablick," – the Dyling with two stars on his turban took a bow – "and this is Gatrum." The Dyling with three stars on his turban also took a bow.

"I understand you want us to help make this room spanking smart again for the elderly people who live here," continued Gawster, "and then they will not have to stay in different homes for long."

"Yes, that's right," replied Ivan, smiling at the terrific threesome.

"OK, let's get to work," said Gawster. "Gablick, Gatrum – the ceiling first I think. If you can all stand back out of the way please, we will begin."

Ivan, Mr Elvic and Benson all moved back and stood in the doorway. Each Dyling let go of their musical instrument and left them to float aimlessly around. Gawster, Gablick and Gatrum turned onto their backs and floated gently up towards the ceiling. They all sucked in their plump cheeks, took a deep breath and started to blow. A freezing wind whipped through the room, followed by clouds of steam that filled the room like a thick fog. Silver dust was falling everywhere. Suddenly, the instruments burst into life, and the Dylings could only just be seen through the disappearing mist, making music again.

"Look! Look at the ceiling – it's *purr*fect again," cried Benson excitedly.

Mr Elvic and Ivan cheered and clapped the Dylings' work. They stopped playing and all took a bow!

"Now for the walls. Let's go for it," shouted Gawster. "Keep well back please, folks."

Mr Elvic and Ivan stepped smartly back as the trombone floated by. Benson peered through Mr Elvic's legs, wondering what was going to happen next. He watched boggle-eyed as the Dylings floated close to the wall. They began to spin, faster and faster, looking like a powerful snowstorm, whistling around the walls. Three times they twisted round the walls, and then came to an abrupt halt, hovering in the air.

"Phew, time for a breather," gasped Gawster, "we are out of practice!"

Much to everyone's amusement, the Dylings floated onto their backs, crossed their arms and closed their eyes! Ivan went to inspect the walls.

"This is brilliant," he exclaimed, "the wallpaper is as good as new. I'm so happy I could cry."

Mr Elvic's face crinkled into a smile as he saw the tears glistening in the young decorator's eyes. He put his arm around Ivan's shoulders, and Benson quickly sprang up, hugging him around his neck.

"All right, all right, you're tickling me, Benson," said Ivan, suddenly going red and feeling rather daft. Benson dropped lightly to the wooden floor, which felt hard to his paws.

"What about the floor? We have no carpet?" he enquired.

"No chandelier either," Mr Elvic reminded them.

"Time for one more tune and then we'll sort that out," came Gawster's voice.

The trumpet, trombone and clarinet were plucked out of the air, and soon Ivan and Mr Elvic were clicking their fingers and swaying to the jaunty tune, and Benson was sitting down trying to clap his front two paws together, at the same time as he was flicking his ears backwards and forwards.

"Now then, what was the carpet like before it was damaged?" asked Gawster, as he finished playing.

"It was a lovely, soft, deep red one with swirly patterns on it," replied Ivan.

"And the chandelier?" enquired Gawster.

"It was beautiful," said Ivan. "There were three circles of glass like raindrops – a big circle at the top and then two smaller ones, with the light hanging in the middle."

"We shall have to see what we can do," replied Gawster, waving his trumpet in the air and then letting go. Gablick and Gatrum let go of their instruments too. The three helpers began to spin again, faster and faster, getting smaller and smaller. Suddenly, like three shooting stars, they disappeared.

Before Ivan, Mr Elvic and Benson had time to draw breath, they were whirling back into the room. A flash of red rippled across the floor, and Mr Elvic quickly picked Benson up as they scuttled out of the way. Light flooded the room as the chandelier came to life, its glass rain droplets gleaming as before.

"Gosh, how have they done that?" said Ivan, "I am most impressed."

"It's magic," laughed Mr Elvic, feeling dizzy with excitement and clutching onto Benson. "Are you OK, little chap?"

"I think so, it's like being in a whirlwind," Benson replied with a chuckle. "These Dylings are fantastic."

Benson jumped down out of Mr Elvic's arms, and his paws sank into the warm red carpet.

"Thank you, thank you so much," said Ivan to the Dylings, "all they have to do now is lift the furniture back in here, and all will be well again."

"Anytime, anytime, perhaps we shall meet again –

I hope so. We've had such a mega time. Come on, let's rock one more time," cried Gawster.

The music beat out louder than ever. Benson lay on his back and waved all four paws about, and Mr Elvic and Ivan decided to do the twist – an old dance move. Suddenly, a movement caught Mr Elvic's eye. He stopped dancing and turned. In the doorway stood Dr Doit and his six elderly residents!! They looked totally stunned at the scene unfolding before them, even Dr Doit couldn't move! Mr Elvic heard the music stop, followed by a whistling sound. He looked and saw the Dylings shooting back inside the teapot at a terrific speed. He watched as the final rush of silver steam disappeared, took one last look at Dr Doit's astounded face and then they were falling – the tunnel of colour snaking out in front of them. Benson was soon practising his aeroplane impressions, and Ivan came tumbling along beside him, clutching his silver wand.

"Why don't you put that in your pocket? It will be safer," called Mr Elvic.

The lights began to fade.

"Hold on, we're nearly back. Get ready for touch-down," he warned Benson and Ivan.

As the tunnel of light vanished, they floated down onto the workshop floor. Ivan pinched himself, looking first at Mr Elvic and then Benson.

"I still don't understand. I feel as if I am dreaming, but I know I am not," he said quietly.

"Benson, will you just pop out and have a look at the moon and the church, please?" asked Mr Elvic, opening the door for him.

"No Ivan, it's not a dream. We have a magical Wishing Machine," he explained to Ivan, grinning.

"A what machine?" cried Ivan. "Tell me all about it."

"Well, it's like this ..."

Benson wrinkled his nose and sniffed the frosty air. It was good to be back. He walked to the end of the lane, sprang up onto Bob's doorstep, and gazed up at the graceful church spire. Once again he sat watching the moon and then made the short walk back to the workshop.

"The moon is about to catch the cockerel," whispered Benson to Mr Elvic, who smiled that smile.

"So you're telling me that the room at Woodhills really is ..." Ivan shook his head and rubbed his eyes. "... Goodness me, is that the time?" he exclaimed, looking at his watch. "So, when will the ladder be ready?"

"Call back in a couple of days, lad – it should be done by then," said Mr Elvic.

"OK, that's fine, 'bye now," called Ivan, making for the door.

He was nearly knocked over by Dr Doit careering in, waving the teapot!

"Oh Mr Elvic, Mr Elvic," he squeaked.

"They've not broken the teapot again, have they?" asked Mr Elvic, smiling.

Dr Doit stopped in his tracks, looking puzzled and ran his hand through his mop of tousled curls. He looked at the teapot and started to inspect it, peering down the spout as if he expected something to come tumbling out.

"I don't really know, I don't really know. Why am I here?" said the puzzled doctor.

"Let's have a look at it," said Mr Elvic, taking the teapot from the doctor's shaking hands. He looked at the hinges on the lid.

"No, they're fine, Dr. Doit. You must have got yourself in a tizwaz over the water damage at Woodhills, and have been working too hard," said Mr Elvic, gently.

"That's just it. Everything is fine and back to normal at Woodhills, and I can't understand how," explained Dr Doit.

"Someone must have done you a big favour, so just be pleased about it and don't ask any more questions," replied Mr Elvic.

"I suppose that's best, that's best," said Dr Doit, shaking his head, "I'm sure you are right, Mr Elvic."

Mr Elvic handed the teapot back to Dr Doit, closing the lid as he did so. "You are a tinker, yes, a tinker, you must have fixed that on when you last mended the lid," laughed the doctor.

Mr Elvic looked down at a silver star winking back at him.

"Perhaps I did," chuckled Mr Elvic, winking at Benson.

"Right, I must be of now, be off. Tea will be ready, goodbye, goodbye," cried the doctor, nearly falling over a lawnmower.

"Cheerio Dr Doit! Don't work too hard," replied Mr Elvic.

Meanwhile, Ivan was waiting for his pizza to be

ready. He dug deep into his pocket to get some money to pay for it.

"Whatever is that?" he thought, pulling out the silver wand. Something special had happened today, but try as he might, Ivan could not remember – perhaps he would one day.

Benson curled up in his usual spot in the armchair and he shivered. The nights were getting very cold now, so perhaps he should try to find somewhere warmer to sleep. He snuggled as far down in the armchair as he could … *and dreamed the dreams that only cats can dream*…

13

NO MORE FREEZING NIGHTS
FOR BENSON

The nights on Cinder Lane were getting colder and colder, as the winter chill began to set in. As the temperature dropped, the moon and stars shone ever brighter in the night sky.

One morning in early December, Benson was woken up by the heavy gritting lorry thundering down the lane, to make the icy road safe for parents dropping their children off at school. With his whiskers frozen, and his body shivering with cold, Benson clambered over Bubble, Squeak and Zimba and jumped off the chair. He had had to make peace with the three brothers, so that they could all huddle together at night to keep warm. Benson made his way through the hole in the fence and into the lane. Frost glistened under paw as he padded along; the icy wind whistled, and, to Benson, it felt as if it was blowing straight through him – he was frozen from the top of his ears to the tip of his tail.

He pressed himself closer to the wall to try and escape from the icy blast. How he missed the warmth of Mrs Tutts' roaring coal fire, and the crackling logs that spat and scorched the fireside rug. Benson felt so miserable that he wanted to cry, and worse was yet to come. The milk on Mr Elvic's doorstep was frozen and the foil lid had lifted up! It looked like a huge ice cream with a hat on.

"Oh no!" thought the poor cat, "I'll even have to wait for the milk to thaw out before I can have a drink."

Light snow began to fall as Benson sat on the step, willing Mr Elvic's car to turn into the lane. Eight o'clock on the dot it appeared. The large headlights looked like dragon's eyes, making their way towards the shivering cat.

"Hello, little chap, you look cold," Mr Elvic greeted him, looking at his friend sitting on the doorstep with his ears drooping.

"I'm frozen, Mr E. Please hurry up and open the door; and look at the milk – it's frozen too!" exclaimed Benson.

"So it is," replied Mr Elvic, picking up the bottle and unlocking the door. "Never mind."

Benson ran through the doorway and across to the wood stove, to see if there were any warm embers left from the previous day.

"Goodness me, you really are cold," said Mr Elvic with a frown on his face, "I am going to have to do something about this."

He rubbed his chin thoughtfully.

"I have an idea, but let's get you warmed up first," he said, putting old newspaper into the stove, lighting it and then putting some wood and logs onto the flames. Benson stood as close as he dared as

130

the wood burst into flames, throwing out some welcome warmth. Mr Elvic lit the umbrella-shaped gas fire that hung from the roof, to spread more heat around the workshop.

"The milk won't take long to thaw," commented Mr Elvic, standing the bottle in Benson's clean bowl to catch any drops of water or milk, and then he unlocked the office door.

Benson turned slowly round, letting the flames fan his cold body.

"Oooh, it's wonderful to feel warm," he cried, beginning to feel happy again. "Mr E., the milk's thawed."

"OK, I'm coming," said a voice from the office.

Mr Elvic came out to pour some milk into Benson's bowl. Wrinkling his nose, he sniffed.

"I can smell burning," he said, looking quickly around the workshop.

"Benson! It's you! You are scorching your fur. Oh, what a horrible smell! Quickly, move away, you daft cat," Mr Elvic shouted.

Benson suddenly felt very hot, and quickly jumped away from the stove.

"Sorry, Mr E., I didn't notice. Luckily you did though," replied Benson, "thanks."

Mr Elvic bent down and scooped the lovable cat up into his arms.

"You smell like a burnt woolly jumper," he chuckled, holding Benson close. "Are you warm enough now?"

"You bet I am," laughed the cat, "all I want now is my breakfast."

After gently putting Benson on the floor, Mr Elvic poured some milk in the bowl, and Benson lapped away merrily. Meanwhile, Mr Elvic was on his knees near the front door.

"Whatever are you doing?" asked Benson, taking a break from his breakfast, and wiping some milk away from his whiskers.

"You'll see soon enough," replied his friend, sounding very secretive.

Benson wandered into the office, away from the wood stove for a while. He could hear Mr Elvic sawing and banging, hammering nails and shouting "Ow" when he hit his fingers. Whatever could he be doing, Benson wondered? It must be important because he knew Mr Elvic had a good deal of work to be getting on with. All of a sudden everything was quiet.

"Thank goodness for that – I might be able to nod off now," thought Benson, settling down under the desk.

"Benson, are you in there?" asked Mr Elvic, pushing open the office door. "I want you to come and look at something."

"Just as I was getting settled," muttered Benson to himself.

"I'm coming," he answered, rousing himself from his quiet spot under the desk.

He followed Mr Elvic to the front door.

"There you are," said Mr Elvic, pointing and smiling proudly, his eyes twinkling behind his glasses. "Try that for size."

Benson looked and could not believe his eyes – A CAT-FLAP! For once he was speechless.

"Well, say something, Benson," laughed Mr Elvic.

"I don't know what to say," whispered Benson in amazement. "You made that for me?"

"Yes, no more freezing winter nights in the furniture yard for you. At least you will be under cover and dry in here," answered Mr Elvic. "You can come and go as you please."

Benson looked at Mr Elvic's kind, caring face, and with an almighty leap, sprang up and hugged him with his two front paws, as best as a cat can hug.

"Hey, steady on, little fellow, you nearly knocked my glasses off. I guess this means that you are happy?" asked Mr Elvic, smiling.

"Thank you so much for sharing your world with me – I am so lucky," replied a very contented ginger cat.

"Now I must get some work done," said Mr Elvic. "You have a go with the cat-flap to see if it works all right."

Benson sprang lightly onto the floor to try out his new door. Mr Elvic went over to the workbench and began tinkering with a machine, grinning to himself every time he heard the cat-flap rattle.

"Whatever do you want a bigger letter box for?" a voice shouted.

Bob had arrived.

"It's not another letter box. It's a cat-flap for Benson to use," explained Mr Elvic.

"A cat-flap for Benson?" cried Bob. "Whatever next? You spoil that cat."

Mr Elvic smiled to himself and said nothing.

"Well, what's wrong with that?" said a voice.

Bob blinked and opened his mouth.

"I said, 'Have you bought a new cap?" spluttered Mr Elvic quickly, looking round to see where Benson was.

"A new cap? I've had the same one for years," exclaimed Bob.

"Then it's about time you had a new one," the voice said.

Bob blinked again and peered closely at Mr Elvic.

"Pardon?" he asked.

"I always thought you had a blue one," gurgled Mr Elvic, trying not to laugh, pretending to look closely at the machine he was working on.

"Whatever is the matter with you today? Making cat-flaps, and thinking I had a blue cap, when I have worn this one for years. Is it something you had for breakfast?"

To his relief, Mr Elvic heard the cat-flap rattle – Benson had gone out before he could cause anymore chaos. He took a huge breath and managed to get his laughter under control.

"Shall we have a mug of coffee and a biscuit before you sweep up today, Bob?"

"What a good idea. Lead the way," replied Bob, thankful that things had returned to normal … for a while at least.

Benson, meanwhile, was sitting on the doorstep in the weak winter sunshine, looking across at the school. He was watching the window to see if Rosie Pendle would wave to him today. After only a few minutes a face appeared, surrounded by a mop of tousled hair, which seemed to be tied up with a ribbon of gold tinsel that shimmered as it caught the pale sunrays. Rosie waved, and Benson could see that she was dressed in white.

"Why on earth is Rosie dressed in white, with gold tinsel for a ribbon at school? Whatever is her mother thinking of? She knows what a mess she gets in!" said Benson to himself, waving back to her with a paw.

"'Bye Mr E., see you tomorrow. Thanks for the coffee," called Bob as he left the workshop.

Without warning, there came the sound of pounding paws, and the rasping sound of heavy breathing. Benson's nose twitched.

"Oh no, it's Dowter on the loose again – where can I go?"

Benson panicked for a moment, and then his green eyes glinted with mischief.

"I'll just sit and wait here."

Dowter the dog hurtled round the corner, bouncing along the pavement like a black kangaroo. Bob flattened himself up against the wall as he thundered past, and then got home as fast as he could. Dowter skidded to a halt as he noticed Benson sitting calmly on the doorstep. Their eyes locked – two pools of green staring at two pools of brown. Dowter's eyes lit up gleefully. Benson had got the better of him last time, now it was his turn. His floppy pink tongue hung out of his mouth, making him look as if he was laughing.

Eyes blazing, Dowter put his head down and charged towards Benson. Benson left it until he could feel the dog's hot breath fanning his whiskers, before shooting through his new cat-flap into the safety of the workshop. There was a crash, followed by an anguished yowl.

"What's going on?" asked a surprised Mr Elvic.

Benson giggled.

"It's only Dowter. He thought he was going to chase me again, but I had other ideas. That cat-flap's brill, Mr E."

"I'd better go and see if he is all right," said Mr Elvic, shaking his head. "I want to nip down to the market in a minute, so you had better stay in here until the coast is clear. I won't be long."

"OK," said Benson, making his way to the wood stove. "I hope Dowter is all right … really!"

Dowter was sitting on the doorstep, rubbing his nose with his paw, his eyes twirling around as if he was seeing stars – where on earth had that cat gone?

"Hello, Dowter, have you escaped again?" said Mr Elvic, coming out of the workshop. He stroked the astonished dog and shook his paw when Dowter waved it at him. "You are just a big softy. You look all right, but that will teach you to chase a clever cat," he chuckled.

"Dowter, Dowter," shouted an anxious voice, "where are you this time?"

Mr Elvic caught hold of Dowter's collar.

"Round here, Mrs Mawks, up the lane. I've got him," shouted Mr Elvic.

Mrs Mawks puffed round the corner.

"Thank you very much, Mr Elvic," she replied, "I don't think the paper-boy shut the gate properly, and the wind blew it wide open. The first sign of freedom and he is off." Dowter was so pleased to see Mrs Mawks, that he leapt up, put his huge paws on her shoulders and covered her with sloppy kisses.

"Come along, you big soft lump, let's get home," she laughed, pushing him down and putting his lead on.

"'Bye Mrs Mawks," called Mr Elvic, as he watched them walk off.

As they rounded the corner, Dowter stopped and looked back, then shook his head as if to say, "what happened?"

Chuckling, Mr Elvic made his way into town and the market.

There was a "plop" as a letter landed on the floor, disturbing Benson from his snooze. He got up, stretched his legs and wandered over to look.

"That's funny, the post has already come today. I wonder what this is," he said to himself, sniffing the light-green envelope. "Certainly nothing to do with food. I hope Mr E. brings me some belly fodder – I'm getting peckish."

He poked his head out of the cat-flap to see if Mr Elvic was in sight.

"Benson, Benson, yoo-hoo," shouted a young shrill voice.

It was Rosie playing in the playground. Benson made sure that the lane was "Dowter free", and that Mrs Gee was not hurtling down on her bike, then walked across the road to see Rosie, who was waiting on the other side of the fence.

Rosie crouched down and whispered excitedly.

"I'm in the Christmas Nativity play, and I'm Gabriel, in charge of the angels. Toby is a shepherd, and Mum and Dad are coming to watch us."

Rosie's big brown eyes were shining with pride.

"I've never been picked to be in a play before," she continued.

"Well done!" Benson whispered, "I'm very pleased for you. I've never seen a Nativity play before. I should love to watch you."

"You're not talking to that cat again, are you?" shouted an amused voice from across the playground – it was Toby, Rosie's brother.

"Oh, I'd better go. See you again soon Benson, bye," Rosie said quietly, and ran off to join her friends playing hopscotch.

Checking that it was safe to do so, Benson padded back across the lane, through his beloved cat-flap and into the warmth of the workshop. He sniffed – what was that fishy smell? His nose led him to a tuna lunch, already in his bowl, in its usual place on the floor near the workbench. Mr Elvic came out from the office.

"I didn't see you come back," said Benson, "you must have crept by."

"You were busy talking to Rosie and didn't see me. She's a good girl, managing to keep our secret."

"Yes, I know. She is so excited because they have asked her to be the Angel Gabriel in the Nativity play, and her brother is being a shepherd," explained Benson.

"That's great!" exclaimed Mr Elvic, "I've had an

invitation to watch the play, to thank me for taking parcels in for the school when they are on holiday."

"That's what the letter was then?" replied Benson. "I should love to see the play, but I won't be able to, I know. Wow! What's that?" he cried, as something near the wood stove caught his eye.

"Go and look," replied Mr Elvic, the wrinkles around his eyes crinkling into a smile.

The excited cat scampered across to the furry object in front of the stove.

"Is it for me?" he gasped, gazing at the round basket-like shape with half a lid on top of it.

"Well, I can't get in it," exclaimed his friend, "try it for size."

Benson touched the inside of the basket with his paw – it was so soft. He quickly scrambled in and cuddled down in the cosy material. It was wonderful!

"It's super, Mr E.," he called. "Absolutely fabulous, what a wonderful day I've had. Thanks … again."

A gentle smile played around Mr Elvic's face. He liked making people happy.

Much later he was getting ready to go home for tea. The workshop was still, and only Benson's contented snores could be heard, coming from the basket.

"Goodnight, Benson," said Mr Elvic, softly, as he locked the workshop door. No one answered.

Benson was *dreaming the dreams that only cats can dream …*

14

THE NATIVITY PLAY

Mr Elvic sat on a front-row chair in the Cinderkids' School Hall, waiting eagerly for the Nativity play to start. He looked very smart today. His mop of white hair was neatly brushed, and he was dressed in his best trousers, jacket and tie. Every so often he pulled at the tie. He didn't like wearing one, but there are occasions when people do have to dress up in their best clothes – and this was one of them. Benson was sulking in his basket in the workshop. He was wondering if he dare go to the school and try to watch the play – surely he could creep in some-how.

Mr Elvic looked around the hall, which was filling up with proud, loving parents coming to support their children in whatever they were doing. Mr Elvic had been told that every child in the school was contributing in some way towards the Nativity play.

An excited buzz went around the hall as the band and choir arrived. Mums and dads strained their necks to wave to their children, although some of the older ones pretended that they had not seen them frantically waving. Goodness gracious, wouldn't they ever learn, embarrassing them like that?

"Come along, Joe, we're going to miss the beginning," a voice said, close to Mr Elvic.

He turned to look, and saw Mr and Mrs Pendle sitting down next to him.

"Hello Mrs Pendle, Mr Pendle. How are you?" asked Mr Elvic.

"Improving, thank you, Mr Elvic," replied Mrs Pendle, "I've just kept an appointment at the hospital for a blood test, that's why we're late. We got held up in the traffic. Would you believe I have to go for the results of the test early on Christmas Eve morning of all days? I don't know what I'll do with Rosie and Toby. They get so bored with waiting around, and Joe has got to take me in the car. I really can't manage on a bus yet, and taxis are so expensive. Oh look, here we go."

Silence fell around the hall as the Nativity play began with Mary and Joseph looking for a place to stay. Mr Elvic hummed along quietly as the children sang "Little Donkey", and a small boy banged two halves of a coconut shell together to make the clip, clop sound of the donkey's hooves.

Benson, who had decided to risk sneaking in, sat watching from behind a curtain on a window sill. A teacher had conveniently opened the window, so that the hall did not get stuffy – just the opening he had been looking for! He was feeling nervous for Rosie, and hoped that she would do well. He could just make out Toby, dressed as a shepherd, carrying a big woollen lamb under his arm, oh, and there was

Rosie looking beautiful in her white angel's dress, with gold-coloured wings and a gold halo – the three other angels had *silver* wings and haloes. Benson watched in wonder, as Rosie pointed to the glittering star and told the shepherds, in a crystal-clear voice, to follow the star, and they would find the new king born that night. The children sang "Twinkle, Twinkle, Little Star" as the angels left the stage, with two girls pinging triangles as they sang.

Rosie stepped forward and looked at her teacher, Miss Silver, who nodded reassuringly at her and smiled encouragingly. She took a deep breath and began to sing "Away in a manger". Benson held his breath as Rosie sang the beautiful hymn, her voice trembling ever so slightly, her face full of concentration. It was all Benson could do to stop himself from cheering as she finished. Just in time he remembered where he was as the other children joined in for the next verse.

Then it was the end, and enthusiastic applause rang round the hall. Mr and Mrs Pendle looked as if they would burst with pride, and Mr Elvic clapped so hard that he made his hands hurt.

"Shoo, shoo, how did you get in here, cat?" a voice shouted, bringing Benson down to earth. He jumped out of the window, fled out into the lane, through the cat-flap and into his basket to dream about the play he had just seen.

Meanwhile, in the school hall, the children were allowed to go and see their parents for a few minutes before they had to go back to their classrooms and wait until it was home time. Their mums and dads were invited to have a cup of tea and a biscuit, and wait for the Christmas raffle to be drawn. Rosie and Toby found their parents.

"Well done, Rosie! Well done, Toby. We are so very proud of you both," said Mrs Pendle, "aren't we, Joe?"

"Yes, very," sniffed Mr Pendle, looking very close to tears of pride.

"You both did very well," said Mr Elvic.

"Oh, hello, Mr Elvic," said Rosie, "I nearly didn't recognise you without your overalls and bobble hat. By the way, how's Benson?"

"Rosie! Don't be cheeky," scolded Mrs Pendle.

"It's all right, Mrs Pendle," replied Mr Elvic, laughing, "Benson is fine, curled up in his new basket keeping warm. I'll tell him all about the play," he added, winking at Rosie, who clapped her hand across her mouth, giggling.

"Mum, it was such good fun being in the Nativity play. Just think, all that happened years ago – I wish Toby and I could have been there," exclaimed Rosie.

"Well, you weren't," laughed her mum, "back to your classroom now. Miss Silver is waiting for you. We'll see you both in a few minutes. You never know, we may have won a raffle prize. Cheerio then, Mr Elvic, nice to talk to you again."

"Oh, sorry. 'Bye," stuttered Mr Elvic.

He had been deep in thought about what Rosie had just said. She wished she had been there on that night when Jesus had been born. Oh, could he make it happen? Did the Wishing Machine hold such powerful magic? He quickly said his "goodbye" and "thank you" to the teachers of the school and hurried back to the workshop, fumbling with the keys in his excitement. The door opened.

"BENSON!" he yelled at the top of his voice.

Poor Benson flew out of his basket, and landed in one leap in a heap amongst the spanners and tools strewn on the workbench.

"I'm sorry, Mr Elvic, I know I shouldn't have, but I did so want to see the Nativity play. If I had known it would have upset you so, I wouldn't have crept in through the open window," spluttered the trembling cat, his ears flying backwards and forwards in double-quick time.

Mr Elvic looked at Benson in astonishment.

"What are you talking about?" he asked.

"I crept in through a window to watch the play, but one of the teachers saw me and shooed me out. I thought they had told you and that's why you shouted my name so loudly," gabbled the cat.

"No, no, oh never mind that. I'm pleased you did manage to see it. It was lovely."

"It certainly was. I wouldn't have missed that for the world," replied a relieved Benson. "Now, why were you shouting so loudly?"

"Well, I was sitting next to Mr and Mrs Pendle, and after the play the children could have a few minutes with their parents. Rosie came across and she suddenly said that she wished she could have been there … I mean at the Nativity, the birth of Jesus …"

"Cor, do you really think we can do it?" asked the astounded cat. "How do we get Rosie to come in here?"

"I don't know … wait a sec … I do!" said Mr Elvic, his eyes twinkling brightly. "Mrs Pendle has to go back to the hospital early on Christmas Eve for the results of her blood test, and doesn't want to take Rosie and Toby in case it's a long wait. It is wish-day Wednesday so I could offer to look after them here – they could bring some toys or books and play in the office, they would be perfectly safe in there, away from the machines. We could ask the Wishing Machine if it could grant the wish. If it could, then they would be here already, if not then we are still helping Mr and Mrs Pendle out – after all, it *is* Christmas."

Benson had been listening very intently and was already feeling a tingle if excitement in his tail.

"I'll walk up to their house in the morning and see what they say," said Mr Elvic, looking at his watch. "Time I wasn't here, my little friend. Time to go and get out of these smart clothes – Mrs E. will be most annoyed if I get oil on them. I wonder what I'm having for tea tonight?"

Mr Elvic checked that the machines were safe and put a couple of logs on the stove.

"That should keep you warm tonight. Sleep tight and sweet dreams," he said, and reached up and switched off the lights.

Benson was sound asleep by the time Mr Elvic had locked the door.

Perhaps he was dreaming of far away places from years ago – *dreaming the dreams that only cats can dream …*

15

ROSIE AND TOBY GO TO BETHLEHEM

"Brrr, it's chilly out there," said Mr Elvic, appearing through the workshop door. Stamping his feet and shaking his body, he sent white snowflakes in a flurry around him.

"Too right it is," said Benson, poking his nose out from his basket. "It began about an hour ago – I nipped out, but not for long. What time are Rosie and Toby arriving?"

"About nine o'clock. Their parents are dropping them off on the way to the hospital, and then they are doing some last-minute Christmas shopping," replied Mr Elvic. "We must hurry up and go into the Rainstar Palace, and see if the Wishing Machine can grant this special wish."

He reached for the keys, and then they both picked their way around the machines to the door that led to the Rainstar Palace.

"Mind how you go down the steps – they might be slippery," warned Mr Elvic.

They were both thrilled at the thought of using the Wishing Machine again – it had been a while

146

since they had been in the Rainstar Palace.

Mr Elvic slid the key in upside down, turned it three times to the right, twice to the left, knocked twice on the knob and the old grey door creaked open.

As they stepped into the Rainstar Palace, small shadowy figures scurried across the floor, running to the safety of their mouse-holes.

A group of stars flew off the velvet cover and fluttered around Benson and Mr Elvic, greeting them like old friends. They smiled at the stars as they floated, some of them landing on them for a second and then taking off again. Mr Elvic waited until they had all floated down to rest on the velvet cover, and then carefully pulled it off the Wishing Machine and laid it over the chair in the corner.

Benson shivered with anticipation, his luminous green eyes fixed on the fantastic machine, hoping desperately that it would grant them this extra-special wish.

"Right, Benson, you know the routine," said Mr Elvic in a hushed voice, "here's hoping that the wish can be granted."

Benson moved forward and placed his paw on the handle. He heard the familiar click and then felt Mr Elvic hold his tail. Once again, the mighty machine began to whirr and tremble, becoming louder and louder, and Benson could feel the handle getting warm. Like a crash of thunder, the machine gave an almighty rumble, and then – silence!

Benson held his breath and waited. The machine began to glow the beautiful deep-red colour, becoming so vivid that Benson thought he would have to shut his eyes – then the light was gone.

There was a rush like the wind, and the machine burst into life. Hundreds, thousands of stars flashing once again through the machine.

"Wish, wish, wish, wish …" came the eerie echo, filling the room with its ghostlike voice. Benson felt the fur stand up on the back of his neck.

"Wishing Machine, this is a very special wish for our friend Rosie and her brother, Toby. Their family has not had much luck lately – their mother has been ill, and their father has lost his job. Rosie was the Angel Gabriel in the school's Nativity play, and Toby was a shepherd. Rosie wished that they could have been there all those years ago on that special night when Jesus was born. Please, are you able to grant this wish?" explained Mr Elvic, in a loud, clear voice. There was silence from the machine, and the stars shooting around it began to blink and fade. Mr Elvic and Benson glanced anxiously at each other. A lump came into Benson's throat. It wasn't going to work – they had upset the Wishing Machine by asking for too much.

Suddenly, there was a tremendous roar, like a waterfall flooding over rocks on a hillside. The stars started to glimmer and glow again, racing faster and faster around the machine, getting brighter and brighter – as bright as they had ever been. Benson hung onto the handle – WHOOSH! The tingling sensation zipped through his paw so strongly that he nearly let go. Stars raced through his paw, down through his tail up to Mr Elvic's arms and back through the other handle that Mr Elvic was holding.

"Yeees," came the whispered voice, "I know of the family and the bad times that they have had, and for this reason I shall grant Rosie's wish, but you must take great care. You will be travelling back in time, into a strange land where you will look very different to the people living there. I do not want to put you in any danger so I shall send the Dylings to help you. As you fly through the tunnel of light look out for them coming towards you. They will bring you clothes so that you can disguise yourselves. Miss them at your peril, because they will only pass you once. Do not forget to catch a star. Now go, my friends, and return safely."

Benson watched as the glittering stars began to fade to just a glimmer, and then they were gone. He and Mr Elvic turned to look at each other.

"Yes, yes, yes! We've done it," shouted Mr Elvic, jumping up and down, and waving his arms in the air.

The big hairy spider, which had swung down to see what all the noise was about, fled back up to his web when he saw the flailing arms.

"No, not quite. We have to catch a star before we go," Benson reminded him.

"Let's go for it then," cried Mr Elvic, walking across to the midnight-blue cover. Taking hold of the corner, he gave it a big shake.

The stars burst into a whirling, swirling cloud of colour, twisting like tiny spinning tops in the air, lighting up the gloom of the Rainstar Palace.

The two friends tried to catch a star but each one spun from their grasp as they got near.

"Oh no, they're landing!" gasped Benson.

The stars began to land gently on the cover, one after the other.

"Quick, Benson, grab one," cried Mr Elvic.

"I am trying, but they dodge out of the way," shouted Benson.

Down all the stars floated, like a shower of glistening raindrops. Soon, there was only one gold star left, hovering above the cover, and about to land.

"Mr E., do something, please," begged Benson.

Mr Elvic knelt down and held out his hand.

"Please, this is for Rosie. She is such a special little girl. Please, star, come to me," pleaded Mr Elvic.

The gold star dipped as if to land, but suddenly rose and gently settled in the palm of his hand.

"Thank you, thank you," whispered Mr Elvic, gratefully. "This means so much to us."

The star winked at him and he took off his hat, and tucked the star safely inside.

"Come along, Benson, we must hurry back and wait for Rosie and Toby to arrive," he said, pulling his hat back on.

Mr Elvic locked the Rainstar Palace door, and he and Benson made their way back up the steps to the workshop.

Inside the Rainstar Palace, a little nose peeped out from a hole and twitched. All was still, all was quiet. The mouse family came out to play.

*   *   *

The workshop door burst open, and in fell the Pendle family, laughing loudly.

"Hello there," grinned Mr Elvic. "What's so funny?"

"We had just got out of our car, and Mrs Gee appeared, trying to ride her bike in the snow. She started to wobble and slide, and ended up charging down the pavement towards us," explained Mr Pendle. "We had to move quickly to get out of her way. I don't know if she made it round the corner or not."

"It's just like dumpling dust," said Rosie, brushing the snowflakes from her coat.

"Dumpling dust?" exclaimed Mr Elvic.

"The snow – my grandma says it looks like the flour she uses to make dumplings to go in the stew," explained Rosie.

"Well, I've not heard that before," said Mr Elvic, chuckling. "Hi there, Toby."

"Hello, Mr Elvic," answered Toby shyly, standing close to his parents, clutching a carrier bag.

He had big, brown eyes, similar to Rosie's, a round face with a turned-up button nose, and dark-brown, unruly hair that looked as if it had a mind of its own.

"Benson," cried Rosie, as she suddenly spotted the ginger cat curled up in his basket.

"Mind the stove," warned Mr Elvic as she rushed across to stroke Benson.

Toby's eyes flashed around the workshop. He had never before seen such weird and wonderful machines. Perhaps he would have fun here after all – it all looked very interesting.

151

"They have brought books to read and puzzles to do," said Mr Pendle, pointing to the carrier bag that Toby was holding.

"Don't you worry. I am sure that we can all keep busy for the day. Now off you go – you don't want to be late for your appointment," replied Mr Elvic.

"Oh, they have brought some sandwiches for their lunch as well. 'Bye then, you two. Be good for Mr Elvic," said Mrs Pendle.

"'Bye, Mum, 'bye, Dad," replied Toby, still gazing round the exciting-looking workshop.

"I said 'goodbye' Rosie!" called Mrs Pendle, laughing at the little girl nearly inside Benson's basket.

"Oh, sorry Mum, 'bye. See you later," said a muffled voice from the basket.

"Mind how you drive in this weather, and there is no need to rush back," Mr Elvic assured them.

"Cheerio Mr Elvic, and thanks again," said Mrs Pendle.

"Looks like it's going to be a white Christmas," called Mr Pendle, opening the workshop door, and helping his wife down the snow-covered step.

"What a lot of different machines you have in here," commented Toby, as the door clicked shut, keeping out the icy wind that was blowing.

"I suppose I have. One day I'll show you what they all do," replied Mr Elvic.

"Why not today?" enquired Toby.

"I think we are all going to be too busy today," said Mr Elvic, with a chuckle. "Now, let's put your bag and coats in the office out of the way."

152

"Rosie, bring your coat to Mr Elvic," Toby called, taking his off.

Rosie obediently took off her coat and gave it to Mr Elvic, who put them both safely in his office.

"Rosie," said Mr Elvic, coming from the office, "can you remember what you wished for after the Nativity play had finished?"

Rosie's nose crinkled with thought, and she looked at Mr Elvic with those big brown eyes. Her face lit up with a huge smile.

"Yes, I remember. I wished that Toby and I could have been there on that special night when Jesus was born,"

"Well, we are going to see if we can make that wish come true," explained Mr Elvic. "There's nothing to be afraid of, I shall look after you both."

Rosie's eyes widened.

"Oh no," thought Toby, "we're not going to be playing silly childish games, are we? I'd rather have been bored at the hospital."

"I want you and Toby to hold hands," continued Mr Elvic.

"Do I have to?" groaned Toby to himself, "I suppose I'd better play along with them. Mr Elvic is kind enough to look after us today." With this thought, he reluctantly took hold of his sister's hand.

Benson crept out from his basket and stood close to Mr Elvic. Rosie's eyes were sparkling with excitement. Was she really going back to that special night? Could it be something to do with that Wishing Machine Benson mentioned sometime ago? She knew that there must be some kind of magic around here because Benson could speak. No, she wasn't afraid, and she couldn't wait for this big adventure to begin. She shivered with excitement.

"It's all right, Rosie, don't be frightened," said Toby, holding her trembling hand.

"I'm not frightened, I'm excited!" Rosie shouted.

"OK, OK, don't shout!" retorted Toby.

Mr Elvic took off his bobble hat and removed the gold star. This time it was Toby's turn to stare open-eyed.

"Rosie, hold out your hand please, palm upwards," said Mr Elvic gently.

Rosie held out her hand, her eyes fixed on the winking gold star.

"Wow," she murmured quietly.

Mr Elvic gently pressed the star into her palm. Mr Elvic and Rosie both froze like snowmen on a winter's day. Toby gasped as a golden glow surrounded his sister and Mr Elvic, like an angel's halo shimmering in the night. Their hands parted and Benson leapt up into Mr Elvic's arms.

"Keep hold of Rosie's hand," shouted Benson to Toby.

Toby gawped at Benson in astonishment – that cat spoke! Before he could say a word, a fountain of glittering stars flowed from the gold star in Rosie's palm.

"This is ace," squealed Rosie, "Mr Elvic, you are so clever. Toby, isn't this fantastic?"

Toby couldn't speak. Could this really be happening?

Stars flashed past him, gleaming and sparkling as

they filled the workshop with their sensational colours, like thousands of coloured sparks from the grinding machine.

"Get ready, here goes," cried Benson, as the tunnel of light began to appear, spiralling up like a huge Christmas tree with racing lights.

"Oooh," squawked Rosie, as she started to tumble through the tunnel.

"Gosh, it's like flying," yelled Toby, clutching Rosie's hand tightly.

"Wheeee, I love this part," shouted Benson, as he zoomed past them, his tail flying straight out behind him.

"You were right, Rosie, that cat can talk," spluttered Toby as they watched Benson rolling over and over, looping the loop as they travelled.

"This is amazing," gasped Rosie.

Toby burst out laughing.

"Look at Benson," he said.

Benson was floating upside down with his legs sticking up in the air. Toby could not resist it any longer. He let go of Rosie's hand, and started to twist and turn. "Superman," he shouted, putting one arm out in from of him, and flying like the super-hero.

"Oh, help," cried Rosie, as she started to roll over and over, "I can't stop."

Mr Elvic reached out and grabbed the little girl's hand in his own. She managed to turn and look up at him, and smiled her most dazzling smile.

"Just relax, Rosie, and let the tunnel of light do all the work," said Mr Elvic, reassuringly. Then he remembered the Dylings were coming through the tunnel with their disguises.

"TOBY!" he shouted, "slow down and let us catch up with you – I've something important to tell you."

Toby flapped his arms as if he were swimming backstroke, while Mr Elvic and Rosie came alongside him.

"Rosie, Toby, we must look out for the Dylings. They are bringing us clothes to disguise ourselves when we reach the end of the tunnel."

"Whatever are the Dylings?" asked an incredulous Toby.

"They are three ghostlike figures, called Gawster, Gablick and Gatrum. Gawster is their leader. We have only one chance to get our disguises from them as they come through the tunnel."

Benson was some way ahead, when he suddenly heard a sound. He stopped still, as if treading water, to listen. With his ears straight up and alert, he could hear strains of vibrant jazzy music echoing along the tunnel.

"I've heard that music before," he mused to himself, "it's the Dylings on their way. I must let Mr E. know."

He put his two front paws around his mouth to make a loud-hailer and bellowed as loud as a cat can bellow.

"The Dylings are on their way. Get ready Mr E., you will hear their music soon."

"I heard you, Benson. Thanks, you smart cat," came the faint reply.

The smart cat watched as the Dylings came into

view, all dressed in gold today, with gold stars gleaming in their turbans. Benson waved a paw as they approached, their gold instruments shining and flashing as they caught the brilliant light of the tunnel. They drew level with Benson, and Gawster waved his trumpet at him.

"Hello there, little cat, nice to see you again. Are the others behind you? We have to deliver these."

He pointed to a gold bag hooked round each of their wispy tails.

"Yes, they are not far behind. Make your music really loud so that they can hear you coming and be ready," called Benson.

"Right chaps! You heard what this little cat said. Turn up the volume!" Gawster commanded.

Benson's tail twitched in time with the music, as with a flourish the Dylings put their instruments to their lips and played their loud jazzy music.

"They are coming. I can hear them," said Mr Elvic to Toby and Rosie.

The children listened and grinned at each other, and gazed in the direction from where the music was pounding. As the music got louder, Mr Elvic could not resist the urge to click his fingers and spin round as if he were dancing. Rosie and Toby giggled, and then gasped in amazement as the Dylings came into view.

"Cool, Mr Elvic, this is so cool," cried Toby, as he tried to take in the picture that was unfolding before him.

Rosie shrieked with laughter at the three Dylings dressed in gold. "Look! They are all playing an instrument – a trumpet, a trombone and a clarinet," she gabbled. "Oompa, oompa, stick it up your jumper."

Mr Elvic had to laugh at the little girl as he was frantically looking for any sign of their disguises. Then he spotted the three gold bags hooked around the Dylings' wispy tails.

"Rosie, Toby. We must unhook the bags from their tails because they will have our disguises in them," he shouted.

The Dylings suddenly seemed to travel faster. Gawster stopped playing.

"Quickly, quickly, grab the bags. Time is running out for us to be here."

Mr Elvic dived across and unhooked the bag from Gawster; Toby did a reverse somersault and retrieved the bag from Gablick; while Rosie dog-paddled and kicked her legs and relieved Gatrum of his bag.

"I've got it! I've got it," she cried, waving the glittering gold bag around her head.

"Rosie, be caref … oh no!"

Too late, Rosie's gold bag was sent hurtling through the tunnel of light, looking like a gold frisbee as it spun. Rosie began to howl, tears flooding down her face. Toby and Mr Elvic looked at each other helplessly – the bag had just disappeared from view. The fading music was replaced by Rosie's wailing.

"Is this what you are howling about?" asked Benson, as they caught up with him.

The gold bag was hanging round his neck.

"It's a good job I saw it coming."

Rosie gave a great sniff and rubbed her eyes, and smiled with delight.

Suddenly, the tunnel of light started to fade, the travellers began to slow down and the light disappeared. They gently floated down and landed on some soft grass. It was pitch dark.

"Let's sit down here for a few minutes while we get our bearings and sort ourselves out," whispered Mr Elvic. "And not too much noise – we don't know who or what is about."

Benson shivered.

They sat and got their breath back, their eyes growing used to the dark.

"I wish someone would turn the lights on," joked Toby.

As if by magic, the full moon appeared from behind a cloud and bathed them in silvery moonlight.

"All you have to do is wish," chuckled Mr Elvic. "Now, let's see where we are."

He stood up and looked around.

"We seem to be on a hillside," he continued, "let's crawl up to the top of that ridge and see what there is. Now, all keep together."

Clutching their gold bags they made their way slowly to the top of the ridge, crawling as quietly as they could. They reached the top and peered over.

"It's the shepherds!" cried Toby.

"Ssshhh!" hissed Mr Elvic. "They mustn't hear us.

"Sorry, I got carried away," whispered Toby.

The shepherds were sitting huddled round a small fire. One person was walking about holding a shepherd's crook in his hand. They could just make out the long dress-like garment he was wearing, and what looked like a tea towel on his head, fastened in place with another band of cloth.

"They are dressed just like I was in the play," whispered Toby, his eyes wide with pride.

A sheep appeared over the ridge, face to face with Benson.

"Aaarrrg," he shrieked in fright, and started to roll back down the hillside.

The shepherds jumped up and started shouting in a funny language, running towards the hillside.

"Quickly, we must find somewhere to hide," gasped Mr Elvic.

They slithered down, not knowing where to go, or what to do.

"Keep together," said Mr Elvic in a loud whisper.

The foreign-sounding voices were getting closer and closer.

"Over here, I'm over here," they heard Benson calling.

They scrambled over, following the direction of Benson's voice, with Mr Elvic holding tightly onto Rosie's hand. Benson was hiding under a huge overhanging boulder, and they all managed to squeeze into the small hidey-hole.

"Gosh, that freaked me out. I'm so sorry," apologised Benson.

"Quiet, all of you!" commanded Mr Elvic, "they're coming."

Huddling together in the darkness, they held their breath, trying not to make a sound. Footsteps rustled through the grass on the hillside, foreign voices

160

chattering loudly – suddenly, very loudly. The shepherds were standing on the very boulder that they were hiding under. After what seemed an age, they decided all was well and made their way back to the warmth of their campfire.

"Phew, that was a close call. Is everybody all right?" asked Mr Elvic quietly.

"I am now," replied Rosie.

"We had better look in our bags and see what disguises we have been given," said Mr Elvic.

Moving from the shadow of their hiding place and into the moonlight, they emptied their bags onto the boulder.

"Shepherd outfits, look," laughed Toby.

"Lets get into them, and then if we are seen we won't look so different. Pull the material well down round your face," said Mr Elvic, "and as for you, Benson, we will have to hide you the best that we can."

Dressed in their disguises, they crawled back to the top of the ridge, with Mr Elvic keeping Benson close to him, not risking any more mishaps. The shepherds were sitting once more around the fire, watching over their flock of sheep.

Without warning,there was a bright light in the sky, and the shepherds flung themselves to the ground in terror. The four travellers watched in wonder.

"It's the angels. It's me and my gang," squeaked Rosie, as the beautiful angels appeared in the sky. Their flowing white robes shimmered against the dark night sky, with their white feathered wings looking like those of a swan.

161

An angel began to speak to the shepherds in a lovely melodious voice.

"That's Gabby," whispered Rosie. "She's telling the shepherds about Baby Jesus being born."

Mr Elvic smiled to himself. "Gabby indeed!"

Gradually, the angels faded away into the dark sky.

"Look, the shepherds are moving," said Mr Elvic, "That young one has a lamb under his arm. They must be on their way to find the baby. Come on, we shall have to follow them, but keep quiet and out of sight."

Stealthily, they followed the shepherds from the hillside onto a dusty track. They kept a safe distance away, and dodged behind rocks whenever they could.

"Look at that splendid star," Benson said, pointing a paw towards it.

"That's it, that's the star over the stable in Bethlehem," Toby said quietly, hardly able to contain his excitement.

They all stood and gazed at the star that was bursting and shining with light.

"Bethlehem can't be too far away," said Mr Elvic. "Look, there it is. You can just make it out."

Straining their eyes, they could just see the shapes of the buildings of the town. A light flickered now and then – perhaps from a lantern. Bethlehem was in sight! Their steps quickened, and Rosie's tummy began to churn with anticipation – they were nearly there!

Soon they were on the outskirts of the town. Mr

Elvic picked up Benson and sat him round his shoulders, under his headdress.

"I think you may be safer up there for a while," he said to his friend.

Benson was grateful. His paws were beginning to feel sore from walking on the dusty road.

Bethlehem was quiet, as they followed the direction of the star, through its small, narrow and dusty streets. Lights glimmered in windows, and some people carried lanterns to light their way. Rosie and Toby were fascinated by the different-shaped houses, and the flowing robes of the people who lived there. Suddenly, Mr Elvic stopped and peered down a narrow street.

"Look, that's where the star is hovering," he said quietly, pointing to a building at the end of the street. "That must be the stable."

"Oooh, I'm so excited," cried Rosie.

"Rosie, shush, don't attract attention," hissed Mr Elvic. "Come on, follow me, quietly now."

Toby's heart began to thump so loudly, he was sure everyone could hear it. The fur on the back of Benson's neck began to prickle. Even Mr Elvic felt nervous!

Creeping down the street, they soon reached the stable door. It was open! Benson jumped lightly down from Mr Elvic's shoulders and peered around the stable door. His tail standing upright, his ears going backwards and forwards, he slipped into the stable.

"Benson! Come back here," said Mr Elvic.

They waited and waited – Benson did not come back.

Footsteps echoed down the street, coming towards them.

"Quickly, hide behind that pile of hay," Mr Elvic whispered urgently.

The three travellers ran and crouched down behind the hay. As the footsteps got closer, Rosie peeped out to see who was passing. She gasped loudly in disbelief – three tall men in splendid, rich-coloured silk clothes, with cloaks encrusted with jewels, and turbans to match, were making their way towards the stable. Without realising, Rosie stood up, mesmerised by the stunning sight. The third man was level with Rosie when he suddenly stopped and looked down at the little girl.

Rosie's eyes widened as the man bent down and patted the astonished girl on the top of her head. He smiled and continued to walk majestically on his way.

"Rosie! What do you think you are doing?" hissed Mr Elvic.

"Did you see them? They were the Wise Men taking their gifts to Jesus. The last one patted me on my head!" squeaked Rosie.

"I wonder where they have left their camels," joked Toby.

"Come on, let's go and watch them give their gifts," urged Rosie.

"Do you think we should? Is it safe?" murmured Mr Elvic.

"This is what we have come for," said Rosie, nearly crying with excitement, "I'm going to look anyway."

There was no stopping Rosie. She ran from behind the pile of hay and stopped still in the open doorway of the stable.

"Let's go and join her," Toby said, with a quavering voice.

Toby held Mr Elvic's hand as they joined Rosie at the stable door. Mr Elvic put a reassuring hand on Rosie's shoulder, as they all gazed at the scene unfolding before them.

The stable was lit by a single lantern. Mary was sitting on a bale of hay, and Joseph was standing behind her. They were both looking tenderly at a baby lying nestled on a bed of hay – the Baby Jesus! The donkey and the other animals were resting behind them at the back of the dingy stable.

Shepherds were kneeling to one side of the manger, and there was Benson sitting with the lamb that they had brought for the new baby.

They watched in awe as the Wise Men gave their gifts of gold, frankincense and myrrh, each bowing to Jesus.

Rosie looked at Mary who gave her a beautiful, radiant smile. She beckoned to Rosie, Toby and Mr Elvic to come forward. With trembling legs, Rosie walked up to the Baby Jesus and knelt by the manger to look at him nestling in the hay. She could not believe what was happening. Mr Elvic and Toby timidly followed and nervously smiled at Jesus and his proud parents. Mr Elvic felt tears prick the back of his eyes. Goodness! Whatever was the matter with him? He sat down with Rosie and Toby, and Benson came to sit on his knee. Mr Elvic gently stroked the soft furry ears. Everything was still. All was tranquil. Time ticked away – nobody spoke. Happiness filled the stable – a timeless picture.

Suddenly, there was a gust of wind that blew out the lantern. The four travellers were back in the tunnel of light, hurling and swirling amongst the stars.

"Make the most of it – we are on our way back home," called Mr Elvic to Rosie and Toby.

"Whheee," yelled the two children as they flew and tumbled through the tunnel holding hands. Mr Elvic stretched out as if he was sleeping, and Benson sat on his middle and had a ride. On they flew through the multi-coloured whirlwind.

"Can you hear some bells jingling?" Toby asked.

Before he could be answered there was another voice.

"Ho, ho, ho," came the voice, and a flash of red shot by. "Don't be late getting home, Rosie and Toby, I'm on my way. Go to bed early and go straight to sleep."

"Was that who I think it was?" asked Toby.

"It must have been – he knew who we were," said Rosie, in a very serious voice.

The light began to dim.

"Get ready to land," shouted Mr Elvic.

As the tunnel of light vanished, they found themselves gently floating down to the workshop floor.

"What an adventure!" cried Toby. "When can we do it again, Mr Elvic?"

"Thank you Mr Elvic," said Rosie, putting her arms around his waist and hugging him. "Oh, our shepherd clothes have gone," she added in amazement.

"So they have," replied Mr Elvic, looking down at his own blue overalls.

"Benson, will you pop out and have a look at the moon and the church?" he continued.

Benson nodded and went out through the cat-flap. The snow was cold to his paws and made him jump. Luckily, Bob had cleaned his doorstep of the 'dumpling dust'.

"Thanks, Bob," he said quietly to himself, as he sprang onto the step. After a few minutes, he heard a car pull up outside the workshop, its tyres crunching in the snow.

That must be the Pendles coming back to pick up their children, he thought. Time to go back.

There was such a commotion going on as he crept back through the cat-flap. Both Rosie and Toby were shouting at their parents.

"We've had a fantastic adventure," said Rosie.

"Benson really can talk," shouted Toby.

"Mr Elvic has a Wishing Machine and has taken us back in time to see Baby Jesus in the manger," squealed Rosie.

"The moon is about to catch the cockerel," whispered Benson from the bench to Mr Elvic.

"Quiet, children! I haven't understood a word of what you are trying to tell me," cried Mrs Pendle, holding her hands up. "Now, one at a time."

"You go first, I can't remember what I was going to say," murmured Toby, looking dazed.

"I can't either," spluttered Rosie, scratching her head.

"I think I must have fallen asleep. I've been

167

dreaming about going to see Baby Jesus," said Toby, trying to grasp at a distant memory.

"You had both nodded off when I looked into the office," said Mr Elvic, winking at Benson.

"Yes, that's it. I had that dream too. How odd! It was wonderful, seeing everybody in the stable. Father Christmas was in it somewhere," chirped Rosie.

"It strikes me that you are both getting too excited about tomorrow," laughed Mrs Pendle. "Anyway, we have something to show you. Your dad and I had an amazing find in the old bookshop today." She pulled a large old book out of her shopping bag. "We were browsing through the books when something gold caught my eye – winking on a shelf in the corner," she continued. "Look, it was a gold star shining on the cover of this book, which is all about the Nativity story."

Something stirred in Rosie's memory. She touched the star with a little pink finger. She had seen that star before – but where?

"And the Nativity scene is very strange," said Mr Pendle.

They all peered at the picture.

"Those two shepherds look just like Toby and Rosie, and the one next to them could be you, Mr Elvic – he even looks as though he has got glasses on. It must be a crinkle in the page – it is a very old book. There's even a ginger cat sitting there," laughed Mr Pendle.

"Amazing," said Mr Elvic, quietly. "Was everything OK at the hospital?" he added, changing the subject.

"Yes, fine, thank you, I don't have to go back anymore," replied Mrs Pendle. "Now, come along, you two, get your coats on, and let's get you home, out from under Mr Elvic's feet."

"It's been a pleasure, Mrs Pendle, no trouble at all," said Mr Elvic.

"All ready then?" asked Mr Pendle, as Rosie and Toby emerged from the office with their coats all buttoned up.

Rosie went to say goodbye to Benson who was in his basket.

"'Bye Benson," she whispered, "I know something magical happened today. Whether it was a dream or not, it was wonderful."

"'Bye, Rosie, have a lovely time tomorrow," whispered Benson.

Toby slowly looked around the workshop, and then at Mr Elvic.

"Mum, can I have another look at the book when we get home?"

"Of course you can, we bought it for you and Rosie," replied Mrs Pendle.

The family left the workshop, shouting "thank you" and "Happy Christmas" to Mr Elvic.

"That's been quite a day, little fellow," he said, pulling Benson's ears. "Time I was on my way."

He quickly checked that all was safe, and threw some logs onto the wood stove.

"'Bye Benson, I'll pop down with your turkey dinner tomorrow. Mrs E. will chitter, but never mind," he called as he locked the door.

Benson watched the flames from the stove flicker

around the walls. He felt warm and safe inside, and soon he was *dreaming the dreams that only cats can dream ...*